# Doreen's 24 HR EAT·GAS·NOW Cafe

*By Reavis Z. Wortham*

**Texas Fish & Game
Publishing Co., L.L.C.**

7600 W. Tidwell, Suite 708
Houston, Texas 77040
713-690-3474

Published by

**Texas Fish & Game
Publishing Co., L.L.C.**

7600 West Tidwell, Suite 708
Houston, Texas 77040
Phone: 713-690-3474
Fax: 713-690-4339
Web: www.fishgame.com

Cover design by Wendy Kipfmiller and Roy Neves.

Cover photo by Donovan Ashley

Chapter illustrations by Mark Mantell.

Edited by Larry Bozka and Judy Rider.

ISBN: 0-929980-09-3

# Dedication

This book is dedicated to all the women of today and yesterday—(*who also loved the outdoors as youngsters, but now stay home with the house and kids*)—who sigh and watch their men walk out the door on hunting trips, fishing trips and the dozens of other outdoor endeavors in which they participate.

It is also dedicated to the love of my life, my wife Shana, and our daughters, the Redhead (Chelsea) and Taz (Megan).

Reavis Z. Wortham
May, 1999

# CONTENTS

Foreword . . . . . . . . . . . . . . . . .vii

Introduction . . . . . . . . . . . . . . . .1

There Oughta Be A Law . . . . . . .7

Adult Toys . . . . . . . . . . . . . . . . .11

Outward
Appearances . . . . . . . . . . . . . .15

Deer Season . . . . . . . . . . . . . . .19

Indecision . . . . . . . . . . . . . . . . .23

Poison Ivy . . . . . . . . . . . . . . . . .27

Spoiled Rotten . . . . . . . . . . . . .31

Busted . . . . . . . . . . . . . . . . . . .35

Lefty . . . . . . . . . . . . . . . . . . . . .39

The Discussion . . . . . . . . . . . . .43

Doreen's Again . . . . . . . . . . . . .47

Fashion Statement . . . . . . . . . . .51

Valentine's Day . . . . . . . . . . . . .55

Cream, Please . . . . . . . . . . . . . .59

Photo Op . . . . . . . . . . . . . . . . .63

Sweet Emotion . . . . . . . . . . . . .67

Listening . . . . . . . . . . . . . . . . . .71

Sad Endings . . . . . . . . . . . . . . .75

Firearms . . . . . . . . . . . . . . . . . .79

Lucky . . . . . . . . . . . . . . . . . . . .83

Boredom . . . . . . . . . . . . . . . . .87

Flavor of the Day . . . . . . . . . . .91

Justice . . . . . . . . . . . . . . . . . . .95

Hooked . . . . . . . . . . . . . . . . . .99

Beepers . . . . . . . . . . . . . . . . .103

Incriminating Evidence . . . . . .107

Freezing . . . . . . . . . . . . . . . . .111

Retirement . . . . . . . . . . . . . . .115

Impending
Wedding . . . . . . . . . . . . . . . .119

Mushrooms . . . . . . . . . . . . . .123

Memories . . . . . . . . . . . . . . . .127

New Truck . . . . . . . . . . . . . . .131

On The Air . . . . . . . . . . . . . . .135

Sunburn . . . . . . . . . . . . . . . . .139

Stingers . . . . . . . . . . . . . . . . .143

Stress . . . . . . . . . . . . . . . . . . .147

Stretched Truths and
Outright Lies . . . . . . . . . . . . .151

Adopt-A-Highway . . . . . . . . .155

Trapping . . . . . . . . . . . . . . . . .159

Remodeling . . . . . . . . . . . . . .163

# Foreword

**WE ALL MAKE MISTAKES.** One of my biggest was encouraging Reavis (rhymes with crevice) Z. Wortham to join the Texas Outdoor Writers Association back in the spring of '92.

Throughout the past 20 years I have enjoyed a mentionable degree of success as a competitor in the TOWA's annual crafts competition, a fact that with all due humility I proferred to Wortham as a thinly veiled challenge. It was, I told him, to his benefit to join this highly esteemed and august gathering of writers, photographers, artists, broadcasters and other ne'er-do-wells so that he might procure an established niche as a serious player in the outdoor media.

I immediately learned two things. One, Reavis Wortham is very seldom serious. Two, he is definitely a player.

He had cold-called a week or two earlier to pitch the idea of writing a humor column for the blatantly fun-resistant publication for which I was editor at the time.

Reavis *Who?*

The name was new, three phone lines were holding and the secretary was out sick. Still, driven by curiosity and knowing that he was already being published in a fair number of newspapers, I asked him to forward some clips.

He did. And it was funny stuff. *Very* funny, in fact.

Proposals for humor columns arrive in the typical magazine editor's mailbox at an average rate of about one a week. Every writer has at least one funny story to tell. Catch is, in the process of telling it said writer almost invariably *tries* to be funny. That is the terminal Kiss of Death to a would-be humor piece.

Fortunately, I had a letter-perfect example from which to make a decision. It—make that "he"—established for me a Ground Zero from which to judge a given writer's "funny factor." His name was Al Eason.

Eason's "Backlashes, Brush and Broken Lines" column, issue after issue was, according to reader surveys, the most eagerly anticipated element of *Texas Fisherman* magazine, for which I served as editor and eventually publisher from late '79 until the spring of '86. After editing Eason's stuff I felt I had a firm baseline. Until I read something as good or better I'd decided to leave the "humor column" concept alone.

The litmus test? If it doesn't make me laugh, I'm not buying it.

I laughed. And although it wasn't until after I became editor of *Texas Fish & Game*® magazine in January of '96, I bought it. Meanwhile, Wortham joined the TOWA and my humor-writing "winning streak" took a precipitous dive. I've placed second or third a few times in the years since, and even took a first in '97. Other than that, though, Rev has pretty well kicked my butt.

Couldn't have happened to a nicer guy (him, not me). But it still makes me wonder about telling him how crafts awards mean so much more when one is competing with top-notch talent. Reavis, suffice it to say, has considerably upped my appreciation factor for framed certificates.

There has, however, been a bright side to the transition. I've gained a treasured friend and confidante. Whenever things get too stressful at the office either I or *Texas Fish & Game*® Managing Editor Judy Rider (who co-edited this book) pick up the phone and give the cowboy-hatted funny guy a call in order to lighten up the prevailing mood.

He never fails us.

Given his occupation as a spokesman for the Garland Independent School District, that's little shy of amazing. You'd have to be holed up in a sealed-off Montana bomb shelter to not know that the atmosphere in today's suburban schools is cautious at the least and downright fear-driven at the worst. Reavis Wortham faces it all with unflagging optimism, the polished demeanor of a veteran administrator and the impervious temperance of a Buddhist monk.

And, perhaps most noteworthy, an absolutely infallible sense of humor.

Rev was the first one to make me laugh after I fractured my right hip via a bizarre accident in May of '98, and the painkillers had nothing to do with my reaction. If the world could be viewed through Reavis Wortham's eyes, Prozac sales would hit rock-bottom.

It's the serious nature of his day job, I suspect, and the need to cope with its endless challenges that fuels the whimsical verbiage Reavis creates when he's away from the professional pressure cooker. That, and a devoted group of long-time fishing and hunting buddies who, through their adventures, mishaps and misdeeds fuel the heartbeat of Doreen's 24 HR Eat Gas Now Café.

As you come to know this motley crew of characters in the following pages, I strongly suspect you'll recognize a few. Not the characters themselves, of course, although most of them do represent actual flesh-and-bone outdoorsmen whose real names Reavis has mercifully omitted. I'm talking about the hunter or hunters in your camp who bear a striking similarity to the likes of Doc, Delbert P. Axelrod, Wrong Willie and the rest of Doreen's irregular regulars.

They're there, in my camp and yours. They are, for those of us who long for the lease months before the season opens, the reasons we care so much. Without them, it'd just be hunting. With them, it's something else.

For that matter, so is Reavis Wortham.

Larry Bozka
Houston, Texas
June, 1999

# Introduction:

## *Doreen's*
## 24 HR
## Eat Gas Now

**THE UNOFFICIAL HUNTING CLUB** has an unofficial meeting place. We frequently stop at Doreen's 24 HR Eat Gas Now Café, which is part of the Conoco station out toward the deer lease. The café is actually at the end of nowhere. It's one of those places frequented by long-haul truckers and local ranchers. The café is close enough to the interstate that truckers don't mind dropping by, but it's also close enough to town to attract adventurous locals.

Most people would like to find a place like Doreen's at least once in their lifetime, but they're few and far between. Occasionally just such an establishment will crop up for those seeking a place to belong, whether it's the donut shop, the corner bar, or maybe the Dairy Queen just off the square. It seems like they appear just when you need them.

The secret isn't just the business, either, it's the fluid clientele, the owner, and of course, the regulars. Sometimes they're sedate and talk quietly, and other times—*depending on the weather*—things can get hot and animated.

Forty years ago, during my larval stages, the meeting place was at

1

Claude's store where the Spit and Whittle Club gathered near the wooden screen door—(*remember how those old doors sounded? Slam...clop...clop*)—and carved on the benches while they told hunting stories or cussed the state of the union. The characters are the same today; they just look different and possess more technology in everything from cell phones to automatic flushing mechanisms in restrooms, which sometimes gets everyone in trouble.

Doreen's Café is a comfortable place, where we can talk and carry on—*most of the time*—without abuse. The stream of patrons is endless, and so are the topics of conversation. Doreen asked me not to give the exact location of her café, not because she doesn't need the business, but because she's afraid if her regulars realize she puts up with all of us they'll quit coming around. It hasn't soaked in yet that the members of the Hunting Club really *are* the majority of her regulars who call the Eat Gas Now our home away from home.

In fact, the café is so close to home that the occasional angry wife, ears laid back, will come directly to the establishment to lead the object of her fury outside by his own ear.

Next door to the station is a small 20-room motel also owned by Doreen. The letters have been gone from the sign for so long that no one but Doreen knows the original name of the place, but apparently no one seems to care. The only legible letters are "OTEL."

Most of the time the little motel is only a quarter full and those are usually hunters who can't stand the thought of camping out another night. So they put up with Doreen's surly attitude for the comfort of *reasonably* clean sheets.

Fifteen years ago Doreen's Café was on the main highway leading out of town, but when the interstate went through most of the traffic went with it. She stays in business because of all the hunters and fishermen who come in to drink coffee and lie, and the old die-hard truckers who still eat Doreen's cooking out of habit only.

We don't go there just for the food. There are only two things in this world Doreen serves that won't kill the average man. Her coffee is near perfection. It's absolute bliss. She uses only Ozark Mountain water. It's delivered every day by a big chrome truck driven by a worn-out old rodeo cowboy named Bum. We're not sure if Bum is his real name or a nickname, but the last time someone asked him if bum was his profession he tried to make the guy drink a whole five-gallon bottle of pure spring water from the *inside* without coming up for air.

Doreen has never, and will never, serve all those fancy flavored coffees which have appeared in everything from bookstores to public bathrooms. It was attempted once, but the results were so unsatisfactory that the uproar that followed put a stop to any further experimentation.

No one has ever had the courage to order anything called an espresso or latté, either. I shudder to think what might happen if they did.

Doreen's other culinary delight is the best chicken-fried steak this side of anywhere. We don't know how she does it, because everything else on the menu is completely inedible. Her fried eggs are so bad ...

*How bad are they?*

... an Exxon gas truck driver once suggested he could use them for tire patches when he's driving on the granite-chip roads in the Northwest Territories. Doreen failed to see the humor in that particular conversation and immediately switched her loyalty to Conoco, which sells her gas without the editorial comments.

Doreen is your typical truck-stop honey. She pops her gum with a snap, which can be heard outside next to the air compressor. She's a tad overweight, just enough to fill out her café uniform. She says that a uniform makes the place what it is. That worries us some.

This is a little disconcerting to patrons who are unaware of Doreen's theory. It isn't unusual to see a family of road-weary travelers enter the Eat Gas Now only to depart seconds later after seeing Doreen emerge from behind the counter holding a greasy rag and wiping egg yolk from the front of what appears to be a nurse's uniform.

She was a cute blonde when she was in high school, but now the general consensus of the gang is that Doreen has a better mustache than most of the male patrons can grow during a four-day weekend.

She also has a large mole on her face, but its placement is a matter of some discussion back down on the lease where we're safely out of earshot. No one can quite agree on the exact location of the mole. It seems to move around from place to place.

One thing we know for sure is that you never, ever, mention her cooking, the mustache or mole where she can hear. John Albert said something once and she physically threw him completely out the door and across the service bay where he came to rest against the Super Unleaded pump in a puddle of fresh transmission fluid. He hasn't been allowed back into the café since. He just stands outside and gazes through the glass windows, huddling in the winter and sweltering in the summer. Sometimes he'll catch snippets of conversation whenever anyone opens the door to enter or leave the café.

John Albert is her brother.

Not all events occur inside Doreen's Café. The parking lot is often the scene of an event or two. We've spent hours simply lounging around a pickup parked on the blacktop, much to her disgust. If we aren't inside, we aren't spending money.

The café is frequently a staging area for upcoming activities. When you have that many outdoorsmen loafing, uh, lounging around inside, someone is sure to come up with an idea of something to do. If that happens we're worse than a bunch of kids. I guess we're big kids in a way, but none of us will ever grow out of it. We don't want to.

Doreen's is usually a stop-off at the end of a day or trip. The regulars will drop by to catch up on the day's hunt or catch, or we'll grab a quick bite at the end of a long day, just so mama doesn't have to cook when we get home.

Many times we stop by just to catch a glimpse of Trixie. She's splendid. More about her later.

So anyway, to get back to my original discussion, we all now stop at the Eat Gas Now on the way to and from the lease, or just when we want to sit around and talk about hunting and fishing. Doreen refuses to allow any discussion about politics, religion, or organized sports in her café, which is just fine with us. If we want politics we can read the paper. We can get religion at church. And with the proliferation of radio talk shows and the 24-hour sports channel, anyone can hear about organized sports any time, day

4

or night.

While we all loaf and compare notes on who shot the biggest buck, there's usually a domino game going on in the back corner near the PONG video game. Willie Nelson—*yes, the Willie Nelson*—has been known to stop by on occasion for a few hands of Forty-two. This sometimes causes problems because one of the members of the Hunting Club is nicknamed Willie and whenever someone refers to "Willie" it's unclear who they're talking about. So now we have Willie *Nelson*, and Wrong Willie.

Example: "When I came in the restaurant Willie was sitting in the back, playing dominos and drinking coffee."

"Willie Nelson here again today?"

"No, wrong Willie. I'm talking about Larry."

Henceforth, Wrong Willie.

No one said the topics were earth shattering, either. The regulars are content to mull over the same old problems they've been working on since 1965. We had to point out the other day how their discussion on Hippies was a moot point, because the only real Hippie left was Timothy Leary and his brain was so fried he thought LSD was a new Japanese import car. When they found out he was dead, a two-hour discussion was required just to hash out a few leftover gripes from the old days.

One Sunday afternoon we were all hip-deep in a discussion over who had taken the biggest rack of the season. John Albert stood outside and shouted through the glass that Delbert P. Axelrod managed to bring in a pretty good four-pointer. At the mention of his name Doreen perked up even though it was John Albert who'd made the comment.

Doreen is sweet on Delbert. No one can understand why. We'd all prefer to use Delbert as cut-bait. We tried to give him to her in payment for a chicken fried one day, but Delbert slipped out of the ropes and got away in his truck before Doreen could get out from behind the counter. She scares him. It could be because her mustache is better than his.

Doc snorted and reminded everyone that Delbert had *run over* the deer with his truck before daylight one morning and so that didn't count.

Wrong Willie scratched his beard. "Jerry Wayne shot an eight-point."

I disagreed. "It was an eight-point only after he found the tine he'd shot off on his first try and glued it back on with Super Glue. I say a seven-pointer just isn't good enough."

"Don got a good six-pointer on opening day," Willie said. "I think he should be recognized for that, and the fact that he's the only guy I've even known who had a dead deer wee-wee all over his khakis."

"I'm not having that kind of talk in my café!" Doreen yelled across the counter. "Not even from a superstar like you, Willie."

See how confusing two Willies can be?

A family of six walked in the door and made a complete turn in unison to get back in their station wagon after hearing all the shouting.

I left while they were arguing. When I go back it'll probably still be the same.

It's good to have some things consistent in your life.

# There Oughta Be A Law

**THE SUN WAS UP. THE FISH WEREN'T BITING.** I'd been with Delbert P. Axelrod, an example of *genus stupidous ignoramus*, for the last seven hours. I needed coffee, desperately.

When we pulled up in front of Doreen's 24 HR Eat Gas Now Café I'd just about had it with Delbert. He was on my last well-frazzled nerve. The café appeared to be packed when we arrived. Cars covered every available inch of the blacktop parking lot. Many were even double-parked.

John Albert was pumping gas into one of those BMs, or maybe it was an EKG, when we got out. "Hi, guys, have any luck?"

"Nope," I answered before Delbert could start telling in great detail about our day from the time his eyes snapped open in his empty head.

We headed for the café. "Watch out! Don't step on that dead bird by the door," John Albert called.

Delbert looked up to see the dead bird.

"It'll be on the ground, Delbert, if it's dead," I explained. "Why is there a dead bird lying in front of the door?" I asked John Albert.

"He must have seen Trixie and tried to get inside."

7

I stopped and waited for an explanation.

"Trixie is Doreen's new waitress," John Albert explained.

Delbert stepped inside and stopped in the door. He clutched his heart and slumped against the doorframe.

"Defibrillator," Doc shouted from the counter. "Someone get the heart paddles. Delbert saw Trixie."

It was our first sighting of Trixie and it will remain with us forever, like the first car we owned, the first buck we shot, or the first time we ever kissed a girl.

Trixie is . . . radiant.

Where Doreen is plain, plump, mustached, and has a mole that travels at whim, Trixie is something to behold. She fills out her uniform.

Lordy.

Watching her walk is a religious experience. Her long curly hair is fire red. Her nails match.

So do her lips, oh, those lips.

Rock-solid southern fire and brimstone preachers break into a cold sweat when she smiles. Trixie is beautiful. Men forget to breathe when she's around.

I stepped over Delbert's slumped body and squeezed in between

Doc and Jerry Wayne at the counter. "Coffee," I croaked.

Doreen glared at us from her perch behind the register. "Drink it, too, Rev. The rest of these deadheads just sit and let theirs get cold. I can't make any money if they don't swallow. At this rate I'll have to let Trixie go before the week is out."

Seventy-two cold coffee cups were raised to numb lips. Perfectly choreographed, 72 Adam's apples bobbed once, twice, and 72 empty cups were held out to Trixie for refills. From above it probably looked like one of those old Esther Williams swimming ballets.

The phone rang behind Doreen. Three cups instantly whistled toward the annoying instrument. Doreen caught two, but her reactions are getting slower.

"Been fishing?" Trixie asked me.

One hundred and forty-four eyes snapped toward me, suddenly insanely jealous because I had attracted Trixie's attention. I was shocked that she spoke to me. "Yeah."

I'm a lady-killer with my swift repartee and snappy wit.

She placed a full cup in front of me and poured in just enough cream. I didn't ask how she knew I used cream. It is simply assumed that Trixie is perfect.

"I love to fish," she said. "I've always wanted to fish in one of those fancy bass rigs you guys use." Her long fingernails absently caressed the back of my hand.

We all stared at the anointed hand.

A full quarter of the café's patrons hit the door at a dead run to be the first one to hitch up his boat.

"Is anyone going to order anything to eat?" Doreen asked in exasperation.

"I'll have a chicken-fried steak," I said.

Delbert staggered up to the counter and took a recently vacated seat. Trixie grinned at him. Her grins can be sold for a thousand bucks each. The corners of her blue eyes crinkle.

Did I mention they're as blue as the sea?

Delbert thumped on his chest a couple of times to keep his heart going. "I'd like to order something to eat," he said.

Trixie leaned her elbows on the counter and leaned toward Delbert. Her eyes crinkled even more. Another bird hit the window and died a satisfied death. "What do you want, cutie?"

"Y'all have any calf fries and eggs?"

We froze in horror, sure we'd heard wrong. But he didn't stop there. For some insane reason Delbert felt he needed to actually *talk* to Trixie. "Have you ever wondered what could have possessed the first man to ever eat those things? Or imagine the first egg ever eaten.

"I can just hear a caveman say, 'Look, that just came out of a chicken's butt; I think I'll eat it.' "

Trixie smiled wider and earned the love of everyone in the place.

But there still oughta be a law against Delbert.

# Adult Toys

**DOREEN'S 24 HR EAT GAS NOW CAFÉ** was full when Delbert P. Axelrod, my personal albatross, and I stepped out of the twilight and into the café.

Squirrel season was on as of that morning and the members of the Hunting Club were in full camo regalia after a hard day in the woods. Squirrel tails were in abundance.

I placed my new toy on the counter in front of Doc, Wrong Willie, and Patrick. Jerry Wayne dozed peacefully in a booth, across the table from two little old blue-haired ladies who whispered quietly to each other, lest they wake him up.

I started to ask why Jerry Wayne was sleeping in a booth, but Doc picked up the rifle and took my attention away from our sleeping partner. "This is the fanciest airgun I've ever seen. Look here, Willie, it even has a scope on it."

"Just got it the other day," I answered. "It's an RWS Model 48 Magnum air rifle. It's made in Germany. The muzzle velocity is over eleven hundred feet per second, which makes it darn close to a .22 caliber rifle."

The members of the Hunting Club were impressed. A crowd gathered, nodding in the appreciation that men share over souped-up BB guns.

"What have you been shooting with it, squirrels?" Wrong Willie asked.

"Me and Delbert have been down at that field not far from the dump. We settled in under the shade and picked off rats for a couple of hours to sight it in. We'll shoot some squirrels with it tomorrow."

"I love to do that," Jerry Wayne mumbled from under his tilted gimme cap. We looked over at the booth. Jerry Wayne was already asleep again. The little ladies nervously huddled together over their coffee, making tinking sounds with their spoons while they watched Jerry Wayne snore.

Doreen came out of the kitchen. "Why do I have firearms on my counter?"

"We were just out shooting and came in for supper, Doreen. Give us whatever you have on special today," Delbert answered. She's sweet on him, so she forgave our little firearm transgression and plopped a glass of tea on the counter.

"Get anything?" Doreen asked.

"Shot about 15 of the little rodents," I answered, and reached for the sugar.

"Where are the tails? You know, you have to have proof," she stated and then handed me a teaspoon so I wouldn't have to stir with my finger.

Her question kinda shocked me. I thought about it for a minute and said, "Well, we didn't cut their tails off."

She snorted. "I hope you guys cleaned them as soon as you got back to the truck. My daddy used to say that they tasted better if they were cleaned as soon as possible."

Conversation in the restaurant came to an abrupt halt. We stared at Doreen for a full minute, waiting for the punchline.

Delbert gulped. "Your daddy *ate* them?"

"Sure. We were raised so far back in the woods that we ate whatever Daddy would shoot. If it wasn't them, we'd eat quail, or possum, ducks, or any varmint he shot and brought in."

The two little old blue-haired ladies rushed from their seats and headed at a totter for the ladies' room.

"Urp," said Delbert and virtually threw himself off the counter stool. His headlong rush carried him between the two little nauseated ladies like a seven-ten split in bowling. They whirled around in place for a moment and then resumed their rush as if it had been nothing more than a windstorm.

"Maybe that's why she looks like she does," Jerry Wayne mumbled from under his cap. He reached out and pulled one of the abandoned coffee cups toward him.

"Doreen, I know times are hard for us all from time to time," I said, "but I'm not sure I'd go around telling that story if I were you."

"Why not?" she asked. "My lands, we've served them enough times in here and you guys didn't say anything. What do you think that stew you're eating was made out of? Remember guys, this café serves a lot of wild game."

Doc mopped his white face. No one moved throughout the café.

"Is that rifle loaded?" Willie asked. "I need to shoot myself."

"You classify this as wild game?" I asked and pointed at my untasted bowl with a spoon.

"I sure didn't trap them in the kitchen, bub."

More patrons hit the door. "What's wrong with everyone?" Doreen complained. "Y'all act like you've never eaten squirrel stew before."

13

The rush immediately stopped. "Squirrel." Willie stated.

"What did you think I was talking about?" Doreen looked at the four of us. "You guys feeling all right?"

"We're fine, now," Doc answered and took a long drink of iced tea.

Doreen threw open the kitchen door and stormed off shouting at James Albert who was looking in from outside the back door. "You'd think those boys were eating *rats* out there the way they were carrying on about a little squirrel head stew."

Delbert had just resumed his place at the counter and was mopping his brow with a shaky hand. "She puts squirrel heads in her rat stew, too?" He asked in a wavering voice.

Doc shook his head and handed me the rifle. "Take this outside and come in again."

I just took it and went on home.

# Outward
# Appearances

THE COLD NORTH WIND DROVE HIGH, dark gray clouds across the sky. The Hunting Club was gathered for lunch in the big circular booth in the northeast corner of Doreen's 24 HR Eat Gas Now Café. We were through eating and were sipping coffee, looking out the window. The sun occasionally broke through the thin clouds, illuminating Doreen's blacktop parking lot.

A white three-quarter-ton diesel Chevy truck pulled into the lot and rumbled to a stop directly in front of our window. Two men emerged from the extended cab, wearing white shirts and ties, and slammed the doors. The driver pointed a remote device toward the truck and electronically locked the doors. The truck yelped and sat quietly.

"Look at that," Woodrow said. "Yuppies driving a Real Truck. I bet that four-wheel-drive monster has never been off the highway."

We examined the clean white truck through the window. The windshield had nary a bug on it, the brush guard on the front was black and unscratched, and the knobby tires were freshly oiled. There were no long, dull scuffmarks in the clear-coat, the sure sign a vehicle has busted brush on a lease. The truck had that Showroom look, yet was clearly two or three years old.

Doc raised a lip. "Shoot. Look at those boys; forty-dollar haircuts, starched shirts and silk Power-Ties. They must have just come from a meet-

ing somewhere. What in the world made them stop here?"

Doreen happened to be walking past. "Just what do you mean by that? Do you guys think only raggedy people like yourselves come in? Maybe they heard about my chicken-fried steak, or maybe my coffee?"

"Then they'd have kept going," Jerry Wayne said under his breath.

"What?" Doreen asked, sharply.

"I said they need to keep going," Jerry Wayne answered, thinking fast. "That rear booth has more privacy."

Doreen left. "Good save," I said.

We high-fived.

The yuppies settled themselves in the booth across the café. The well-fed portion of the duo talked in a loud voice. "And then I told Travis that he should have faxed the stats to me, because I could have scanned them into my laptop computer and would have been ready when the C.E.O. called me on the cellular."

"I think I'm going to be sick," Wrong Willie said.

"Is this what our world is coming to?" Doc asked.

"I'm afraid so," Woodrow said. "Look out in that parking lot. It's full of legitimate trucks covered with scratches and dents, with mud up the sides and the beds full of hay and feed sacks. It's embarrassing that something like that magazine advertisement monstrosity is in our parking lot, driven by two people who can't go to the bathroom without wearing a pager."

"Why do people buy off-road trucks like that?" Woodrow asked. "Most of them don't ever drive on anything but concrete as long as they own them."

"Because it's the *in* thing to do," Doc said.

"People don't say in or cool anymore," I informed him.

"Let's split," Jerry Wayne said. "The longer I stay around people like that the more likely some of it will rub off on one of us and we'll be wanting to wear pleated pants to the deer stand."

"No one says 'split' anymore, either," I said.

We left, to Doreen's apparent relief, and walked outside. The yuppie owners had parked the big three-quarter-ton next to Doc's Greenvan, forcing us to walk past the white truck.

"There should be a law to make people who look like those two buy sedans instead of trucks," I said, looking into the back of the pickup expecting to see an unblemished bed.

"Good lord, looky there," Doc said.

We stopped and were awed to see the heavily used truck bed covered with empty shotgun shells, a motor for a deer feeder, a roll of camo

17

netting, coolers and camp supplies.

"Cool," I said, forgetting what was In.

"I knew those boys were all right," Doc said, unlocking Greenvan with a key. "The minute they sat down and ordered coffee I could tell they were outdoorsmen."

"Fine gentlemen," we agreed, tightened our own ties and slipped sports jackets on over starched white shirts to head back to the office for an afternoon meeting.

# Deer
# Season

**DOREEN'S 24 HR EAT GAS NOW CAFÉ WAS PACKED** solid with successful deer hunters...and five not-so-successful outdoorsmen.

The members of the Hunting Club sat in moody silence amid the revelry of hungry camouflaged hunters. Doc was the only one not depressed over not yet having shot a deer. The rest of us tried to put on a Happy Face.

"I can't believe I didn't see anything larger than a cocker spaniel," I complained.

Trixie brought coffee to our booth. "Poor little feller," she said and ran long fingernails along the back of my neck. Trixie the redheaded waitress is...magnificent. "You'll get one later."

She left and we loved her with our eyes. Everyone sighed.

"You didn't get anything because you spent all morning asleep up there in your tripod stand," Wrong Willie accused.

"Did not," I answered, always the quick wit.

"Did too. Admit it. When I walked up behind you about ten o'clock you were sound asleep with your head down on your chest."

"Well, I was just resting my eyes."

19

"You were resting your eyes so loud I had to see where the snoring sounds were coming from," Wrong Willie answered.

"That was only because I couldn't sleep last night from all you other guys snoring."

"Willie you're not going to shoot a deer if you're out wandering around," Doc said. "You should stay in your stand and let the deer come to *you.*"

"I think I had a dwarf deer walk past my stand," Patrick said. "It was so small it looked like an African dik-dik."

"Watch your language!" Doreen warned from behind the counter. "Here comes my sweetie."

She was talking about watching Delbert P. Axelrod's arrival. He is also known as Bacteria Brain. He screeched his new little sports car into the parking lot and hurried inside. "*I got a deer!*" he shouted and did the Happy Dance.

We sighed. There is no justice in the world.

"Let's see it," Doc said and we escorted Delbert out the front door, followed by most of the café's patrons. If Delbert tagged a deer, everyone wanted to see it.

The group stopped and stared at Delbert's two-seater car as if we'd been flash-frozen. A small four-point buck was seat-belted upright in the passenger seat of the car, with his right foreleg hanging over the side in a rather rakish manner.

Oh no, that wasn't what stopped us. We couldn't believe it when the deer turned its head and looked at us.

"It's still *alive,*" Jerry Wayne whispered, "and it's riding *shotgun!*"

"It can't be," Delbert argued. "I hit that thing so hard with the car it was knocked forty feet. It was deader than one of Doreen's chicken-fried steaks when I belted it in."

"I thought you said you shot a deer," I accused.

"I said I *got* a deer."

"It's tagged," Patrick said, awed. "In the front seat. You tagged a *roadkill.*"

"It wouldn't fit in the trunk," Delbert said defensively.

"It's not a roadkill," I said. "The blamed thing isn't dead, it's still alive."

"When it gets over feeling bad..." Doc began.

He was interrupted when the unharmed deer completely regained

its senses and proceeded to kick the living dogwater out of the dashboard. For some unknown reason Doc rushed to the car, reached in and released the seatbelt. The deer braced its back feet against what was left of the passenger seat, planted his forelegs on the door and leaped out, hitting Doc squarely on the tip of his nose with its head. We all agreed it sounded like someone dropped a raw egg into a mixing bowl.

The deer ran off down the street, Doc's eyes watered, Doreen called 911, and paramedics eventually examined Doc's rapidly swelling nose. They pronounced it unbroken and went inside for coffee. She later said she called 911 for the deer, not Doc.

We heard the police eventually ran down the deer, recovered Delbert's tag and released the only deer in history with seatbelt burns on his stomach.

The only thing we learned about the experience is Doc's later promulgation. "Getting hit in the nose like that hurts so bad that water squirts out of seven orifices."

We learn something every day.

# Indecision

**DOC GOT OUT OF GREENVAN AND PULLED** A huge duffel bag onto the ground. "I need you guys to help me," he said with a frantic look in his eyes.

The Hunting Club gathered around him in the shade. We watched with interest as he untied the duffel and began pulling out assorted pieces of outdoor apparel.

"What do you think?" He held up a battered pair of tennis shoes and two low-top hiking boots.

We stared and waited. Something wasn't right, but we couldn't figure out what it was. Doc frowned at the shoes in his hands.

"Well?"

Patrick cleared his throat. "Well what? All I see are two pairs of shoes."

Doc snorted in exasperation and waved the shoes. "Which pair? *Which pair*? I can't decide which shoes to wear with these khaki shorts. I simply can't go fishing in something that doesn't match."

We squinted. Jerry Wayne edged toward the lake and possible

escape in its watery depths.

"You feeling all right, Doc?" I asked.

"Of course I'm all right. All I'm saying is if these hiking boots don't look good with my new shorts I'll have to wear tennis shoes. Is it too much to ask you guys for an opinion. Dang. I may as well go back to town and shop for a couple of more days."

"I like them both," volunteered Wrong Willie. He's always game for a good conversation.

"That doesn't help," Doc complained. "You would have been no help when I was trying to decide which T-shirt to wear, either, with that attitude. If it hadn't been for the salesman I'd probably be standing here in only my drawers."

We shuddered in unison.

"That's cute," Wrong Willie gave in. "Where did you get those shorts?"

Doc smiled in relief. "*See?* Someone understands. I bought them at Wal-Mart."

Patrick stared at him suspiciously. "Why are you helping him in this nonsense?"

"Because it's not nonsense. Everyone likes to look good when they're out. Just ask any woman. It takes them thirty minutes to decide which lipstick to wear while they're vacuuming. Doc is simply becoming one of the masses."

"But he's a male," Jerry Wayne moaned piteously. "What's this world coming to?"

During our brief conversation Doc was rummaging through the duffel. "Which cap, then?"

He held out two gimme caps.

Neither matched his Wardrobe Of The Moment.

I carefully examined him to see if Martians had somehow bored a hole in his head to let all his brains leak out.

"Maybe I'll wear jeans instead." Doc changed into a pair of faded jeans. "Do these make my bottom look too wide?" He twisted around, trying to see his backside.

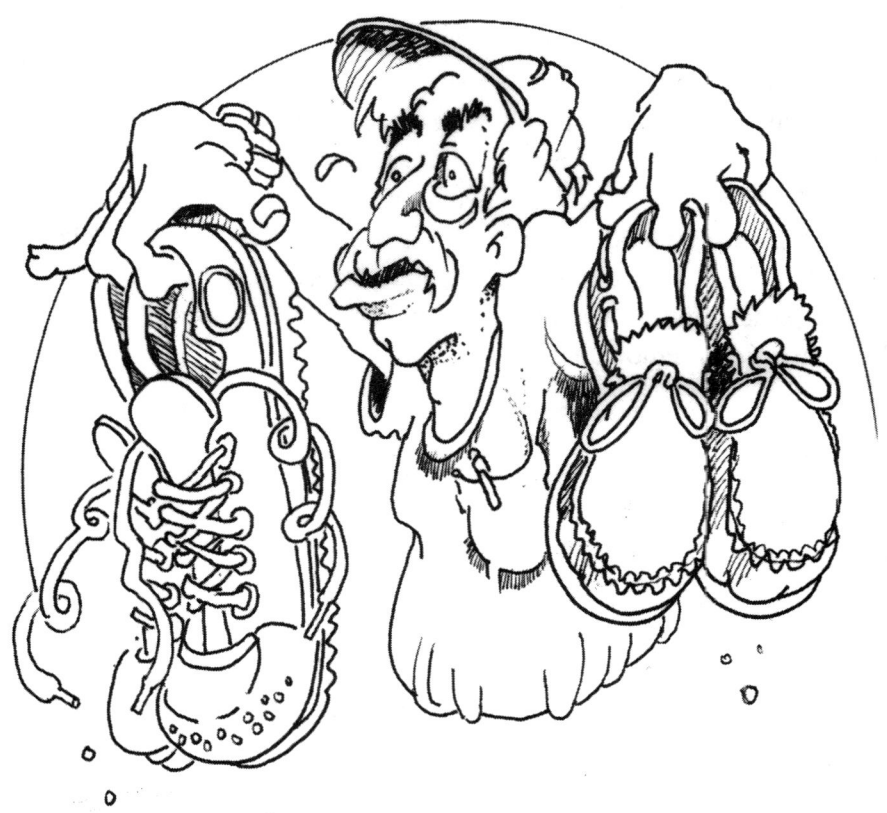

I swallowed a gag. "They're fine. Whichever you like."

Doc flushed. "Don't do me that way. Maybe if these jeans had pleats I'd look thinner."

"It's a good thing it isn't hunting season," Jerry Wayne said. "If his camo patterns didn't match it would be worse than this."

"I was thinking about that," Doc said. He reached into his duffel once more. "I really don't like mixing patterns. Here, I wore these on opening day last year. Do you think anyone would notice if I wore them again, and just changed hats?"

"We need a doctor," I said and reached for Doc's arm.

A loud crash in the kitchen woke me up. I realized I'd been dozing on the counter at Doreen's 24 HR Eat Gas Now Café.

"You all right?" Doc asked, concerned. "You were moaning and drooling on the counter."

I almost hugged him in relief, but stopped just in time. "Man. I was having a bad dream about you and clothes."

Delbert P. Axelrod, a moving inanimate object, emerged from Doreen's bathroom holding two pairs of shoes. "Which shoes for tonight on the boat? Deck shoes, or tennis shoes? I can't decide."

"Lead boots would be best, and thirty feet of water," I said, and closed my eyes to enjoy the thought.

# Poison Ivy

**"WHY IS HE PINK?" DOREEN ASKED TRIXIE.**

The 24 HR Eat Gas Now Café was full at noon on the opening day of deer season. Fully camouflaged hunters slurped coffee and tried to chase the chill from underneath several layers of thermals and ragged insulated coveralls.

Trixie frowned at Delbert P. Axelrod, whose family would have benefited by draining the gene pool before he was ever born. His hands, arms, and most of his face were covered with a dry, crusty pink substance. He huddled miserably on the farthest stool and didn't move.

"He shot a deer," she said, nonchalantly. "That's all the guys can tell me because every time someone says anything they all start laughing."

"Of course," Doreen replied, sarcastically.

Everyone in the café broke out in laughter, spitting coffee into the air in a large brown mist.

"*See?*"

I emptied my cup and held it out to Doreen. She refilled. "I'm waiting for an answer," she said.

"Why am I always the one to get sucked into these conversations?" I complained. "I'm irritated about deer season. I didn't even see a deer track, let alone a whole deer."

"Because I asked you, that's why."

"Are you related to my mother?"

"Do you want to stay outside with John Albert?"

I looked through the plate glass window and saw John Albert, Doreen's brother, who had long ago been banished to forever stay outside the café and pump gas or on occasion quickly slurp a cup of coffee in extremely cold weather, because he'd once mentioned her mustache. He huddled against the wind and gazed forlornly into the café.

I waved. He waved back.

Forlornly.

I took a moment to compose myself. "Delbert had a little problem," I said and snorted with laughter into my coffee. The café broke up again. Delbert, silent, looked miserable.

Delbert had experienced a phenomenon I'd heard of all my life, but had never encountered. He'd shot a deer that had been browsing in poison ivy. Deer love poison ivy, and in the fall will actually seek it out to eat the scarlet, orange and yellow leaves.

"He shot himself a deer eating poison ivy. What's worse, he made a good shot, the best he's ever made. His deer fell stone dead, right in the thickest stand of poison ivy in the county. Then Fuzzhead there," I pointed at Delbert, "didn't know what poison ivy looked like."

"I do now. I couldn't help it though," Delbert whined. "You guys quit laughing. I'm itching all over."

With all the laughing the café sounded like one of those preppy comedy clubs.

Doreen stared at Delbert, sympathy for "her man" oozing like thick syrup. Made me want to gag.

"I pulled him out of the vines to clean him," Delbert said. "I suspicioned it was poison ivy, so I didn't touch any of the leaves. No one has ever told me that the oil from that stuff can get on a deer and be transferred to someone who's just cleaning him."

"Look on the bright side," Doreen told Delbert. "You could have gotten it worse. You could have rubbed your chest and stomach."

We nearly hit the floor. Jerry Wayne laughed so hard his face turned red and we began to think he was going to vapor-lock. His laugh turned into a gag and he stopped only after turning blue. We pounded on his back for a while until the danger had passed.

"Oh, it's worse, isn't it Delbert?" I asked, wheezing with laughter. "Still itching?"

He looked embarrassed.

"How can it be worse?" Doreen asked.

"It's worse all right. Go on Delbert," Doc prodded. "Tell everyone how it could be worse."

He sulled up and glared around the café. We snickered. Eyes bugged out from mirth. Doreen and Trixie leaned over the counter in anticipation.

"Because," Delbert said quietly, "I drank so much coffee this morning that right after I finished cleaning the deer I had to go to the bathroom. And that's right, *everything* itches."

Understanding dawned on the girls' faces. Then embarrassment.

We didn't hear anything else, because most of the café patrons were on the floor, laughing.

# Spoiled
# Rotten

**DOC RAN THROUGH THE ICE-COLD RAIN** and entered Doreen's 24 HR Eat Gas Now Café in a spray of frigid water. Most of the Hunting Club looked up in surprise. Everyone except Delbert P. Axelrod, my personal enigma, had been in the café since the first raindrops began to fall.

"I've seen everything," Doc said in disgust. He settled onto a stool and picked up the cup of coffee Doreen had poured as soon as she saw him pull up in Greenvan. "I'll never hunt with another one of Don's dogs again."

We seldom hear Doc make such rash statements, especially when he knows I'm nearby and will be sure to use anything he says in an upcoming column.

Willie leaned over the counter so he could see Doc past the members of the Hunting Club who were lined up like targets on an arcade shooting gallery.

"Get it off your chest," he said.

"Why did you leave Delbert out in the rain?" Doreen interrupted. She still has a crush on Delbert, though most of us think this is a result of inhaling too much of the wax she uses on her mustache. "He's out in the

31

rain fiddling with your dog trailer."

Doc never turned around. "He's fine. I'm not his daddy. Besides, he needs to feed that dog out there, because if I get near him again I'm going to strangle him."

"Delbert?" I asked hopefully.

"No, the dog. Don kept telling me how great his pointer was so I thought I'd give him a try. I was going to take him for a couple of passes before I came by here to pick you guys up."

He stopped, went to the door, opened it and shouted at the dog trailer. "But I'm never going to hunt with a prima donna dog again!!!"

Delbert, who's always been high strung, flinched at this outburst and looked ready to run. Several new patrons of the café edged away from the rest of us. They eyed Doc warily, since most people aren't used to Crazy People shouting at dog trailers.

They obviously weren't quail hunters, because quail hunters frequently shout at inanimate objects.

"I should have known I'd have trouble with this dog when Don told me he flies a plane to wherever he wants to hunt, instead of driving. They've been doing it for the last couple of years, but I didn't think it would make a difference in how the dog would hunt.

"So here we are, at the edge of a field, when I opened the door ..." he stopped, went to the café's door, opened it, and shouted at the trailer again. "He refused to come out because we drove instead of flying!!! I don't own an airplane, and I refuse to buy or rent a plane just so a spoiled *dog* will hunt!!!"

Through the rain-splattered glass I saw Delbert flinch at Doc's shout.

Jerry Wayne ordered a chicken-fried steak and rested his cheek on a fist. "I still don't see why you're so upset. We've had dogs that wouldn't hunt before."

Doc stomped over and plopped back down on the stool. Three people left half-finished meals and hurried out into the rain, lest the Crazy Man commence shouting at them.

"You haven't heard the end of the story," Doc continued. He started to get up again, but Doreen placed her hand on his as she refilled his cup.

"I managed to coax this spoiled dog out of the trailer. He looked at the mud and growled like he was upset that I had the audacity to want to hunt in wet weather.

"But, after a little while he put his nose to the ground and started hunting. In no time at all this," he paused, "this *animal*, pointed a covey of

33

birds. I was so unnerved by then that when the birds flushed I missed three easy shots."

Knowing his mood, we all looked sorrowfully at our saucers.

"Boys, that dog looked at me like I'd grown an extra head. Then he turned and in less than three minutes found another covey. When they flushed I missed three more times."

Before we knew it Doc was back at the door. He looked around the café. "And because I missed six straight shots that dog from hell lifted his leg on me, turned around, and ran back to the truck. When I got there he was behind the wheel and had the doors locked. I'm gonna kill him!" Doc charged out the door. We boiled out after him, to try and save the cost of a good bird dog.

Delbert took one look at all of us spilling out the door on the run and assumed he'd done something wrong. He rushed to the cab of the truck and pulled frantically on the door handle. The doors were locked, and the spoiled bird dog sat in the cab where it was warm and dry.

We assured Delbert we weren't after him, this time, and he crawled into the dog box where he could huddle in peace. The rain came down harder. I gave up and went back inside. Doreen stood at the window, looking out at the group of wet hunters gathered around the truck.

"This is the first time I've ever seen hunters with their noses pressed against the *outside* of a truck."

"You've obviously never hunted with a spoiled bird dog," I answered and shivered as a cold stream of water ran down my back.

"More coffee?"

# Busted

**"THIS TIME OF THE YEAR IS ALWAYS HARD ON ME,"** Jerry Wayne announced.

Doreen poured a warm-up for everyone at our table in Doreen's 24 HR Eat Gas Now Café. "I know," she sighed. "It's rough on me, too. No one has any money during Christmas. Yesterday I only made fifty dollars in tips and Trixie only made a hundred and seventy-five."

We frowned. Doc found a pen and began to add on a paper napkin.

I was surprised myself. Trixie should have earned more than that. I made a mental note to leave *two* dimes on the table when we left.

We looked at Trixie at the counter. She favored us with a splendid Trixie smile. Several weaker hearts almost failed.

"Christmas always takes all our money," complained Delbert P. Axelrod, Fishbrain Boy. "I'm broke. By the time I bought everyone a present my bank account was flat. I barely have money to eat. What's the special today?" he asked Doreen.

"Personal size pizzas," Trixie called from the counter.

"I'll take one," Delbert said. "I'm not too hungry today. Just cut it into six slices instead of eight."

Doc frowned again and began to divide.

Patrick sipped his coffee. "Give me a couple of donuts."

"No," I said. "You're not supposed to have the sugar."

"All right. Just give me a dozen donut holes."

"That's better."

Doc frowned harder and multiplied. He ran out of napkin-space and reached for another.

The rest of us ordered coffee and nothing else. Money was tight.

"I know what you mean," Patrick continued. "By the time I bought mama a complete makeover at Neiman's I was out of money, too. I don't know what we're going to use to pay the rent."

"You think a makeover will do any good?" Delbert asked.

"Naw. Wrong Willie gave one to his wife last year and she still looks the same."

"You're gonna get letters if you use that one," Wrong Willie told me.

"My problem is the kids," I said. "By the time we buy bikes, microscopes, clothes and four-foot tall Barbie dolls, I barely have enough money for shotgun shells."

"Well, Christmas is for kids," Doreen said. "Enjoy it now, while they still believe in Santa. I wish you guys would buy something else here, though, besides coffee. I need the money to get a present for Trixie."

From nowhere a hat plopped into the middle of the table and dollar bills rained from every corner of the café. It made Doreen mad and she went to sulk behind the counter.

We continued to lament the lack of funds until Doak Hopkins entered the café with a rifle case in hand. He plopped it on the counter, flicked the lock and opened the lid. Inside lay a shiny, unmarred Weatherby 7mm Mag. We gathered around and drooled.

"I have to sell this old rifle," Doak said. "I need some more money for Christmas."

"How much?" Doc asked.

"I'm in a bind. I'll take three hundred."

A particularly nasty scuffle broke out among cash bearers and those

waving checkbooks. Doc won out and admired his newly purchased rifle.

Doreen was livid. "I thought you guys said you were all broke! You've all been moaning about not having any money and now everyone suddenly has enough cash for a *rifle?* Y'all said you didn't even have money to order *food*!!!"

Doc closed the case. "Dang Doreen, if we wanted to eat, we'd go home."

Wrong Willie looked around the parking lot. "How did we get out here?"

"By not being destitute," I said, and we left.

# Lefty

**THE HUNTING CLUB WAS HUDDLED AROUND** the big round corner table in Doreen's 24 HR Eat Gas Now Café. We were looking at a map of our hunting lease in East Texas. Wrong Willie had gotten it off the Internet. Technology had arrived for the Club.

"What's that?" I asked, pointing at a straight line.

"It's the highline wire going through the lease. This darn map has everything."

Doc's attention was divided between our map and the couple in the booth next to us. They'd snuggled up in the seat behind ours and were making goo-goo eyes at each other. "Do you love me, honey?" she asked.

He sort of glanced over at us and sighed. "Of course I do, baby-cakes."

Wrong Willie stifled a retch. "Right here is where your deer stand is, Rev. And this broad line is the highway."

I looked at the line, surprised at how close the highway was to my stand. We could actually see the little draw below where I was hunting, and the ridge below which I was sure the deer would follow.

The couple's conversation turned more serious. We couldn't help overhearing what was being said. "If I die before you," she asked, "would you bring your new girlfriend to our house?"

We cringed. He handled it well.

"No darling. I couldn't live in a house full of your memories. I'd have to sell it and live in an apartment."

The Club sighed. "What are all these hatchmarks?" I asked Wrong Willie, pointing to a section that looked to be less than half a mile from my stand.

"It looks like the checkering on a gunstock," Doc said.

"Those are little roads. I just found out there's a housing addition just on the other side of those trees."

I thought about how easy it would be for an unscrupulous hunter to step across the road and hunt our lease.

"If I died before you, darling," continued the lady, "would you let your new girlfriend drive my car?"

She was making us nervous and I was concerned. Her husband wasn't paying close enough attention to their conversation and was trying to see the map on our table without being noticed.

"No dear," he answered, a little too fast if you asked me. "I couldn't bear to look at your car and remember your delicate hands on the wheel. I'd sell it and donate the money to a charity in your name."

I was getting nauseous. Doreen and Trixie, who is....sumptuous, were eating it up. They leaned over the counter and sighed.

"You mean those houses and all that traffic are only a few hundred yards from where we're hunting?" I asked, trying not to listen to the conversation behind us.

"Yup," said Wrong Willie. "You can't tell the houses are there from the road, and when we were driving around looking at the lease, no one thought to investigate that side of the highway. Looks like we're hunting in the suburbs."

"No wonder I haven't seen much deer sign out there," I mused.

"And darling," she continued. "If I die before you, would you find a new girlfriend and take her fishing with my bamboo flyrod?"

"Not at all," he answered, really getting into making her feel good. "I'd put the flyrod on the wall so I could see it each evening as I sat by the fire and remembered the good times we had on those Colorado mountain streams."

Every lady in the café sighed at such a romantic notion.

"We're not going to see a deer this year," I said. "Look, there's an entire cluster of trailer houses not half a mile from Doc's stand."

"And darling," she continued. "If I die before you, would you let your new girlfriend shoot my Remington 20 gauge?"

"Naw," he said without thinking, distracted by our map. "She's left handed. The shell would eject across in front of herrrrrrrrrrrrr."

The explosion behind us was short and vicious. The guy frowned at his rapidly disappearing wife and all the women glaring at him from around the café.

Doc turned and faced him. "Darling, since you're gonna be alone this season, wanna buy out our part of the deer lease?"

"Can I live there, too?"

"Sure," I answered and handed him the map. "Pick out a trailer."

# The Discussion

THE HUNTING CLUB SAT IN THE WARM COMFORT of Doreen's 24 HR Eat Gas Now Café and watched sleet periodically rattle off the trucks outside.

I knew there was an ominous feeling about the day. My hunch was right when I looked through the window and saw John Quinn waddle through the falling ice toward the café.

"Uh, oh," I said. "Let's get out of here."

Doc turned looked up from the domino game and winced. "Doreen. Is the back door unlocked?"

She looked up and continued wiping at the counter. "You guys be nice to John; he's sweet."

John Quinn is a nice enough guy, I guess. He loves to hunt quail. But his most favorite pastime is telling hunting stories. All right, you ask, what's wrong with that?

The answer is simple. John doesn't know how to tell a story. He gets started on one idea, wanders around in conversation for a while and skews off onto about four different topics before he wraps up his story.

43

By the time he's finished I've forgotten what he was talking about in the first place.

"Howdy boys," John said and settled his considerable bulk onto a stool. "Conversation is kinda quiet in here today. It reminds me of a quail hunt last year with some of the boys down near Archer City."

Without a word Doreen carried a fresh pot of coffee around to everyone in the café. She knew from experience that no one would get a word in edgewise while John was talking.

The sounds of blowing and sipping began to fill the café as we cooled coffee.

"There were supposed to be more birds in that part of the country than they'd had in twenty years. Well, we weren't really at Archer City, we were a little ways out of town with Dave Tomes and his brother Woosie.

"You know those boys. They made their money in oil and never did a lick of work in their lives after that. Old Woosie is different. He has bad table manners, hates country music, and used to spend most of his time riding around in that little blue truck of his, cussing imported cars and trying his best to tear it up on those dirt roads around his place so he could buy a full-size Ford truck.

"I don't think he ever wore that little truck out, though. He went to San Antonio one weekend and parked it in a hotel parking lot. When he came out the next morning it was gone. The only thing left in his parking space was a peeled-off Gilley's bumper sticker."

"How many birds did you . . ." Willie started and was then cut off.

"I wonder how anyone can live in Central Texas and not like country music," John pondered. "I spent a lot of time there when I was a kid. We didn't have much. We were so poor that Daddy had to take out a loan to pay attention."

I looked around at all the glassy eyes staring at John.

"Woosie would get up in the morning, start drinking vodka, and would drive around all day, running off the road and trying to hit blackbirds sitting on the shoulder. Hated blackbirds. Thought they were a lower life form than lawyers."

"After the truck was stolen?" Doc asked.

John looked surprised that anyone was left in the café. "Why no. That was before the truck was stolen. Three or four of us piled in the back of the truck with Dave, and Woosie drove us over to a place he said was full of birds.

"I didn't like the looks of the place, because someone had rootplowed a hundred acres or so. I don't know why birds will hang around somewhere like that, but Woosie was convinced we'd get our limits that day."

I completely zoned out. The domino game continued unabated, but no one paid any attention. I was daydreaming about big game hunting in Africa. I didn't notice when Doreen refilled my cup again.

I took a drink. Coffee the temperature of the sun seared through my mouth and parboiled my tongue.

I sprayed everything in front of me, including the local constable comfortably napping in the booth beside me.

He woke up with a screech. I looked at Doreen for help. Doc's head slipped off his fist as he took that moment to doze. His chin landed with a thump on the counter.

John stopped.

Delbert P. Axelrod, my personal source of constant unpleasantness did what Delbert does best. "Why does this café remind you of bird hunting that day, John?"

"Why, because I was hunting with some fellows just like y'all," John smiled, pleased that someone was still listening to him. "Well, mostly they were older, and . . ."

Doreen quietly unlocked the back door. I was the first one out.

# Doreen's Again

**DOREEN'S 24 HR EAT GAS NOW** Café was full when I shivered my way inside. John Albert, Doreen's banished brother, stood in the alcove and huddled against the wind.

"She ever gonna let you back inside?" I asked.

"I'm moving up," he grinned. "A week ago she wouldn't let me get *this* close."

"Just don't make any more cracks about her mustache," I advised. "I'll send you some coffee."

John Albert grinned. "Thanks. At least the coffee is free while I'm out here."

Doreen plunked two cups down on the Formica counter before I could say anything. "I know," she snorted. "You said you'd send him a cup, just like the rest of your bunch."

I didn't answer. I knew better. John Albert had his cup and I huddled around mine in a matter of seconds. The Hunting Club held its usual council near the jukebox.

The conversation seemed to be teetering on the lighter side for once.

"What with warmer weather coming up I was over at the fishing store the

other day," Doc pontificated. "You know, seeing if they had something that I couldn't live without."

He looked at me. "Before you say anything, I already know most lures are designed to catch the fisherman and not the fish. But they have a new one that I think is a good idea."

We waited. Doc sipped his scalding coffee. "This new lure is called The Redman." He cast his literary lure out on the water.

"I haven't heard of that one," I said. Club members around the table nodded and frowned; they obviously hadn't either. "Is it a topwater or a diver?" I eyed his imaginary cast.

"Neither," Doc answered. "It's just a package of little tiny plugs of chewing tobacco. All you have to do is drop a few over the side of the boat and wait about ten or fifteen minutes."

"You're kidding," I bit like a nearsighted bass. "Then what?"

Doc leaned back in his chair. "Well you fool, when the fish come up to spit you hit them with the oar."

The table roared around me. I'd walked into that one as blind as a bat. From the way everyone looked around and laughed I knew I wasn't the only one to get hit with *that* hook today. That's what happens when you come in late with this group.

February is a completely unpredictable month. There are still a couple of seasons open, but for the most part hunting is over. The weather never seems to cooperate, it's either sleeting or the south wind is blowing so hard it will swamp a boat in five minutes. So we tend to gather at Doreen's and talk about hunting or fishing until we can get out on the water once again.

"How are your dogs doing now that all they have to do is lay around and get fat?" Theo asked Doc. I looked past his shoulder and saw John Albert standing inside the door for the first time in five months.

"They're doing fine, except for the fact that Junior and White Dog spend half their time snarling at each other."

I glanced at Doreen who appeared to be engrossed in a paperback novel. Occasionally she'd reach up and stroke her upper lip. I shook my head at John Albert when he looked like he wanted to say something.

"They used to get along," Doc continued, "slept in the same kennel and ate out of the same pan, until last week. But late the other night, and I mean late as in two in the morning, I never heard such a racket in all my life.

"I went outside in nothing but my drawers and saw the worst dog fight I've seen in years. Because it was so cold I'd put all five dogs in the same house so they'd stay warm. Well, someone must have committed some minor indiscretion because all five of them were tangled up in the worst knock-down drag-out you can imagine.

"They were so mixed up I couldn't tell where one dog ended and another began. I hurried and got me a shovel, meaning to pry them apart, but it didn't do any good. We all fought for about five minutes. Every time I'd get two of them apart the rest of them would start again.

"The funny thing was that after I worked on them for a few minutes they all moved the fight inside the doghouse like they wanted to get away from me. I dropped the shovel to go get the water hose and when I got back I saw the funniest thing I've ever seen.

"You never heard such snarling, squalling and thumping like I heard in that dog house. Then, just when I was ready to spray them with water here came old Junior, sneaking out of the fight on his belly. It looked like one of those old westerns where the sidekick crawls out of the saloon brawl on his hands and knees.

"I was waiting so Junior could get out of the way when White Dog and one of the others grabbed him and dragged him back inside to the war. Junior's eyes widened and his front toenails left scratch marks all the way back inside the house."

We broke up. Even Doreen was laughing.

Wrong Willie went for more coffee. "Well, did you stop the fight?"

"Yeah, finally. You never saw such a sorry bunch of dogs the next morning. It looked like they'd tangled with a weed eater. The vet said there wouldn't be any lasting damage though. But everyone has their own kennel now."

John Albert settled slowly down between Doc and myself. He was inside. Then he blew it.

"Hey, have any of you guys ever wondered why you never see any *old* Hari Krishna's selling flowers in the airports?"

I thought it was a good question.

Doreen didn't, though. Maybe John Albert can come back inside next year.

# Fashion Statement

**I KNEW WE WERE IN TROUBLE** that particular winter's day when the Hunting Club trooped into Doreen's 24 HR Eat Gas Now Café and encountered a new glaring waitress. She was there to temporarily replace Trixie, who as I've repeatedly said, is . . . splendid.

It didn't help matters much that Jerry Wayne had perched upon his head like a two-day-old road kill, a toboggan of such horrific construction that none of the Club members deigned to mention its lethal ugliness for fear some ancient Toboggan Curse would cause us to all wish for such head coverings.

An astigmatic 120-year-old grandmother had apparently knit the cap. It was overly tall for a knit cap, and stiff enough that it stood straight up as if Jerry Wayne was smuggling dead cats underneath.

Of the two top corners—*yes this knit cap had corners*—the foremost was an inch or so higher than the rear, making it look three feet tall.

It was yellow, with green reindeer.

The new waitress who was only in Doreen's for a couple of days while Trixie recovered from a fishing trip with Delbert P. Axelrod, one of nature's more horrible mistakes, summed up the hat situation with two words.

"Nice hat," she said, rolling her eyes and suppressing a gag.

Having never seen the lady before that moment we looked up from the counter. Jerry Wayne was shocked. He stared at the offending waitress' oversprayed head. "Thanks," he responded hesitantly. "You like it?"

"It's *you*. Is it supposed to look like that?" she asked.

"You're new," Delbert stated.

Jerry Wayne patted his head in an effort to get a grip on the conversation already light-years ahead of him. "Of course it's supposed to look like this. I bought it."

"That figures. You could get jail time for that thing."

"You want me to take it off?" he asked, trying desperately to restore some authority to the conversation.

"What? So I'll have to look at your old messed-up hair all the time you're in here? No! Besides, that thing shouldn't be left lying around."

Club members began to back away from the target of dissension.

"Who *are* you?" Jerry Wayne asked in frustration.

"Candy. I'm Doreen's sister."

"I thought I recognized your mustache . . ." Delbert began and then to his credit, for the first time in his life, realized the potential danger and shut up.

"Are you *mad* about something?" Jerry Wayne asked. "Where's Trixie?"

That was a mistake. "Why?" Candy asked. "Do you think she's a better waitress or *prettier* or something?"

I gulped and glanced at the door to be sure it wasn't obstructed.

"Or something. Let's try this again." Jerry Wayne said. "We were just out hunting and came in for lunch."

"The dogs spend all their time pointing that cap?"

"What's wrong with my hat?" Jerry Wayne asked, more frustrated than ever.

"It's not a hat, it's a cap. It's really a toboggan. It looks like something you'd see in Timothy Leary's ski nightmares."

"Doreen!" Doc called.

She arrived, annoyed to have been bothered. "Nice hat, Jerry Wayne."

He ripped the offending piece of apparel from his head and flung it onto the floor.

"Comb your hair," Doreen said.

"You wouldn't have to look at it if your new waitress hadn't been ugly to me."

"What do you guys want?" Candy asked.

"Coffee," we answered.

"And a chicken sandwich without the mayo," Jerry Wayne interjected.

"Watching that fat?" Candy asked.

"Naw, you're not *that* big," Jerry Wayne answered.

I closed my eyes and sighed as the battle loudly moved outside. "How did you stay out of this one?" Doc asked me.

"By thinking pure thoughts," I said. "I think I'm going to start hanging around McDonald's, though."

# Valentine's Day

WRONG WILLIE RUBBED SLOWLY ON THE odd-shaped light-bulb in his hand. Scattered across the corner table in Doreen's 24 HR Eat Gas Now Café were the disassembled parts of his million-and-a-half candle-power predator light.

I slid into the booth across from him and waved at Trixie. She smiled back. The entire café sighed. "What's the matter with your nite-lite?" I asked, wondering where the rest of the Hunting Club was hiding out. "Where is everyone?"

Wrong Willie scratched the bulb with a putty knife. "I lost the red lens for my light."

"All right," I answered. "I'll bite. What happened?"

"Delbert sat on it and broke the darn thing the other night while we were hunting coyotes," Wrong Willie said. "So in desperation we decided to make a red lens to continue the hunt."

He quit talking and rubbed some more.

"And?" I prompted.

"All we could find was the red wrapping paper off a box of Valentine

55

candy. It sounded like a good idea."

"*And*," I jigged him again.

"It didn't work. When about two hundred and fifty-thousand of the million-and-a-half candles were lighting up, the red cover burst into flame

and melted onto everything. Looked like a baked chicken."

"Sooo?"

"So without a light we couldn't hunt."

Doreen brought me a cup of coffee and mumbled some snide comment about the café not being a repair shop.

"Why is this story so hard to get out of you?" I asked.

Wrong Willie presented me with the saddest look I've ever seen. "Well, we gave up and went home. When my wife asked me about the hunt I told her that same story."

I waited.

"When I got to the part about using the red paper off the box of Valentine candy she reminded me, rather harshly I might add, that I hadn't given her any candy this year and she wanted to know who the devil I'd given it to."

"Oh," was all I could say.

"She wouldn't accept my explanation that the red candy paper came from a box Delbert was eating. She thought I'd given it to some other woman."

"So what did you do?"

"I gave up. There's no reasoning with an angry woman. And the frustration was that she didn't look mad. That's when I said I just wished that God had made women like horses."

"This has got to be good," I said.

"I just mentioned they could lay their ears back like horses when they get mad and then we'd know it."

"You didn't know she was mad?"

"I couldn't see her ears. I knew she was mad when she threw the light at me."

We looked at the pieces scattered across the table.

"So where is Delbert and the rest of the guys?"

"Delbert is out looking for a red lens to replace this one."

"And the rest of the guys?"

"Out buying Valentine candy for their wives after I told them this same story."

Delbert P. Axelrod, a horrible misstep on the evolutionary ladder, bounded through the door. *"I found one,"* he shouted and then took off for the rear exit, skimming a red object in our direction.

He was through the back door only seconds before an irate truck driver ran in behind him. "Where is that little creep?" he shouted.

Everyone in the café pointed to the back door; forget loyalty. "What are you after him for?" I asked as he rushed past.

"He took the red taillight off the back of my rig!"

The café fell silent, which was broken several minutes later by

Wrong Willie. "Dang. This won't fit. I hope the guys have better luck finding candy for their wives."

I looked out the window as they drove up, hangdog expressions on all. "What's the date?" I asked.

"February 16."

"They didn't," I answered. Trixie smiled at them when they came through the door and everything was all right, as long as they were in the café.

# Cream, Please

**DOREEN'S 24 HR EAT GAS NOW** Café was busy for a Saturday morning before daylight. I was surrounded by several members of the Hunting Club, drinking coffee and listening the National Weather Service on the radio.

Our plans to be on the lake at sunup were scrambled due to the gale-force winds that were trying to tear down Doreen's sign. It was only four in the morning, but the café was rapidly filling up with frustrated fishermen and bleary-eyed farmers. Maybe it was bleary-eyed fishermen and frustrated farmers.

"I can't believe you ran out of cream," complained Delbert P. Axelrod, who suffers from a terminal case of intelligence repellent. "What kind of café is this?"

Doreen's mustache began to bristle. It's the consensus of the Hunting Club that she has a better mustache than most of us could grow on a two-week vacation.

"It's the kind of café that would be a lot quieter if you weren't here," she snapped. "Why don't you go outside and complain to John Albert; he's the only one who cares if you're happy or not."

Doc ignored the exchange and carefully poured coffee from his cup into the saucer on the counter. He blew across the coffee's surface to cool it off. Doreen's café is one of the few places left in this world where you can still slurp your coffee like your granddad once did.

Sometimes it's hard to hear the jukebox from all the slurping going on up and down the counter. I once heard an unsuspecting tourist complain that the café sounded like a convention of sinus sufferers. She left, retching, but I'm still not sure if it was from the sounds or Doreen's cooking.

Doc finished his saucer and looked at the parking lot through the huge windows. It was lit only by the glow from the Eat Gas Now sign. "Doreen, it wouldn't hurt you to put some lights out on that parking lot so we could see. If I needed to get anything out of my boat I'd have to wait until daylight."

He's the only person I know who can talk to Doreen like that and still stay in the café. She just poured more coffee into his cup and increased the volume on her weather radio.

"Don't you have some powdered cream somewhere?" Delbert whined.

"Why is he here?" Doc asked me.

I shrugged and tried to look like I didn't know Delbert. The wind pushed Floyd Gibbons through the door. He struggled to keep it from slamming and overheard the last exchange.

"Delbert, I've got an old milk cow out in the trailer. I'm taking her to the sale barn, but if you've got a notion to go out there you can get a little milk from her for your coffee," he offered.

"You may as well," I said. "We're not getting on the lake this morning. I imagine we'll just drink coffee and go home later."

Delbert took a water glass from the counter and headed for the door. "I can't believe I have to milk a cow just to lighten my coffee."

"Do you know how to milk a cow?" I asked.

"Of course. All you have to do is grab one and squeeze."

"There's plenty of room inside the trailer," Floyd instructed. "Just

MANTELL

climb in and fill 'er up."

Doc had already forgotten Delbert before he was out the door. He began telling about the time he'd accidentally performed a bodily function on an electric fence.

I watched John Albert join Delbert and together they disappeared behind a trailer in the dark parking lot.

"I walked like John Wayne for a month," Doc concluded.

I didn't hear the laughter. I was up and hurrying to open the door for John Albert, who was half carrying Delbert's tattered remains into the café. His shirt was torn to shreds, his eye was black, and he was covered in dirt from his head to his shoe. The only thing on the other foot was his sock.

We dumped his useless carcass on the hastily cleared counter. "What happened?" Doreen shouted. "You look like you've been swarmed by a roll of barbed wire."

"That thing almost *killed* me," Delbert gasped. He held the shards of the water glass in a trembling hand. "I thought you said she was a gentle old milk cow."

Floyd frowned. "She is, son. She never acted that way with me."

I looked through the window at the parking lot. Cattle trailers were parked on each end of the dim lot. "What color is your trailer, Floyd?" I asked.

"Blue."

"I went to the gray one," Delbert shuddered and twitched.

A grizzled old rancher walked up to the register to pay his bill. "That was mine, and I ain't hauling milk cows."

Doc glanced up from Delbert's terror-stricken eyes. "What are you hauling?"

"Rodeo bulls."

I smiled. "Just grab one and squeeze, huh?"

Delbert twitched some more.

All in all, it was a good morning for the rest of us.

# Photo Op

**"WHAT ARE YOU GUYS LOOKING AT?"** Doreen asked. We had dozens of photographs spread across the counter of Doreen's 24 HR Eat Gas Now Café.

"Don't end a sentence with a preposition," Doc instructed, not looking up from a rather badly focused photo.

"All right," she said. "Let me rephrase it. What are you guys looking at, bonehead?"

"We're looking at pictures we took during the last year," I said quickly, before a fight could break out. "I think I'd like to send a shot to a magazine, if we can find something we like. Just think, a photo by one of us on the cover of *Texas Fish & Game*."

"How about this one?" asked Delbert P. Axelrod, Idiot Savant. He held up a photo of the deer he'd taken this season.

The Hunting Club examined the photo. "Good shot of that eight-point," Jerry Wayne said.

"It's focused well. Everything is sharp as a tack," said Patrick.

"Good lighting," said Doreen.

I looked closer. "Good try, guys. But the tire tracks from the eigh-teen-wheeler that hit him take away from the overall outdoor experience."

Wrong Willie picked out the next photo. "How 'bout an action shot? Here's one I got of Rev when we were hunting that wild boar. Look," he pointed to the huge hog. Its long tusks gleamed with a brilliant white sheen. "This is a great shot of the charging hog."

Doc snorted. "The hog may look good, but Rev is kinda fuzzy climbing that mesquite tree to get away."

"I wanted to shoot him from above," I defended. "How does my hair look?"

"It's sticking straight up. You were scared," Delbert commented.

"Not! I don't want to talk about it. I'm still not healed up from all those thorn punctures."

"How about this picture of the deer camp?" Patrick suggested. "This has meaning, mood, and it makes a statement. But they may not like it because of all the woodsmoke around Doc's head."

"That isn't smoke, it's mosquitoes," Doc said. Everyone scratched sympathetically.

I selected a photo. "Here's a nice shot of Wrong Willie standing on the roof of the truck, filling the feeders on the lease. Course he looks a little blurred, too, like he's moving."

"He is. I like this second one better, where he's hitting the ground," Delbert said.

"Naw," Patrick said. "The best one is where he's laying on the emergency room table with that pretty nurse leaning over him."

We examined the nurse.

"You guys are missing the point," I said. "We want something to go on the cover of a magazine, not a hospital shot."

"Here's one!" Doreen said. "Look at the size of that fish!"

We all looked closely and sadly shook our heads. "No, that isn't a fish," Doc said. "It's a picture of a minnow through my new magnifying lens. See? That big blue thing beside it isn't a cooler, it's the thumbnail I hit with a hammer."

"How about something simple?" Doreen suggested. "Here's a nice picture of a fishing fly."

"No!" I said. Everyone looked at me expectantly. "Because that's a Yellow Humpy and it's stuck in my ear. The nurse at the emergency room took that one."

"Don't talk nasty," Doreen said.

"I didn't. Humpy is the name of the fly. Look, there's the back of my ear, and my hair."

"Who is this!!!???" Doc asked, surprised he hadn't seen this picture before.

"The nurse that helped, see, there it is between her fingers."

"This is the one!" Wrong Willie shouted. "She's beautiful, it's a properly exposed shot, and it's outdoors oriented. You can see the fly she's holding."

"Barely," I began. "This isn't what they want. They want..."

"Huzzah!" everyone shouted and hurried out to the post office to mail the picture to *Texas Fish & Game*.

Doreen glared at me. "Well, it *is* a Humpy," I said, and held out my empty cup.

"Don't talk nasty," Doreen snapped and poured coffee over my hand and the rest of the pictures.

# Sweet Emotion

**THE AIR OUTSIDE OF DOREEN'S 24 HR EAT GAS NOW** Café was hazy and thick, reminding one of Los Angeles smog or the poker room in a college frat house. It was nothing but pollen, but more than I'd ever seen during any particular season.

Doreen's Café was packed with allergen-laden, red-eyed would-be fishermen lamenting the end of hunting season. Everyone was affected by the airborne particles. Sinus problems were rampant. There was so much sniffling and eye watering going on it looked like a wake.

Jerry Wayne reclined in a booth with his head tilted back and his mouth wide open. He carefully applied eyedrops to his irritated orbs and was so engrossed in his activity that he didn't notice two other members of the Hunting Club trying to arch empty peanut hulls into his open mouth. For some reason an open mouth seems to beg for such competition.

Doc and Wrong Willie were busy rubbing their eyes and honking noses, their own of course. Doreen bustled throughout the café, her mouth in a tight line. She hated this time of the year because of the liquid sounds coming from her regulars. She's forever accusing us of running off the higher quality folks who drop in from time to time for a chick-en-fried steak.

She prefers we suffer in silence.

Delbert P. Axelrod, a man who's picture we'd love to see on a milk carton, came in brandishing one-half of what would have been a 12-point rack.

"Hey guys, look what I found up behind Rev's stand!" he held up the shed antler and shouted as if we were all stone deaf. "Rev must have missed this old boy during one of his naps."

I glared at Delbert, trying to wish him up to the North Pole.

He thumped the antler down on the table, knocking over several unplayed dominos in the process. I perked up, excited by the possibility that an annoyed player would attempt to perform an anatomically impossible maneuver upon Delbert's person with the antler.

However, Delbert has become such a nuisance that Wrong Willie simply swatted the antler away as if a two-pound mosquito had landed on the game. He played the double nickel and scored twenty points. Delbert sat down and leaned his chair back on two legs.

"I need more medicine," Doc said, sniffling. "This time of the year is killing me."

He leaned over and searched behind the counter for a tissue, or any available cloth.

John Henry blew. "You know, on top of everything else I didn't even get to hunt turkey this year."

Wrong Willie unscrewed the cap off a tube of nasal spray while he waited for his next turn. He irrigated a nostril and then wiped his eyes.

"Do that somewhere else," Doreen snapped.

A grizzled old rancher entered the café and looked around at the red-eyed members of the Club. He settled onto the end of the counter, glanced at the antler in Delbert's lap, ordered coffee and listened quietly.

Doreen wasn't happy with any of us.

"You guys are driving me nuts. All you do is hang around here all day and moan about the end of hunting season. I've almost had it with all of you. Y'all can hunt again the first of September. Why don't you go fishing or something?"

"It's worse outside," I sniffled and instantly regretted it.

"There is no way it could be worse outside. You guys sound like a bunch of old women, weeping and carrying on like someone broke your best set of teacups. Go...*home!*"

"There's been so much rain (sniff) that all the streams are out of their banks. We can't fish because it's too windy, and it's too humid (sniff) to camp. At least the weather isn't such a factor when we're hunting."

"This season was a disappointment," Jerry Wayne said, rapidly blinking tears from his eyes. "I only went bird hunting two or three times (sniff) and I didn't even see a deer this year."

"The pheasant hunt was fun in December (sniff)," Doc said and wiped his eyes. "But it only lasted for one weekend. I didn't get out as much as I wanted."

He blew.

"No one did," I answered and wiped my eyes. I wondered when my sinus pill would kick in. "I needed more (sniff) cold weather and a lot more hunting."

Wrong Willie blew again and shuffled the dominos. "This was a pretty good year, though, for ducks and geese (sniff). I'd like to be duck hunting right now."

"I guess we could go down to the creek and put out a couple of cane poles, but I sure hate to go out feeling like this," I said, sniffling.

"I just don't think I can take it right now," Wrong Willie said. He wiped a tear.

"You wish y'all had this antler," Delbert teased the players.

"I don't think I can take much more of this," Doreen grumbled. "I've had it with all you little babies." Exasperated, she looked at the rancher and refilled his coffee cup. "Isn't this something?" she asked.

Delbert took that moment to lean a little too far back in his chair and upset his precarious balance. He went over, kicking the domino table in the process, knocking the antler across the table, scattering the game and scalding the players with several just-filled cups of coffee.

Screeches of indignation filled the café. With practiced agility, Delbert grabbed his deer antler and shot out the café door.

"Gimme that antler!!!" Wrong Willie shouted at Delbert. He had every intention of beating him to death with it. They streaked past the old rancher, followed by several other steaming hunters brandishing various blunt instruments and assorted cutlery.

The rancher looked around at the rest of us who elected to stay in out of the pollen. "You know, I don't believe I've ever seen grown men take the end of hunting season so hard. The way they were sniffling and weeping makes me think these youngsters are more emotional these days."

He paid for his coffee and walked across the silent café full of sniffling outdoorsmen. He looked at Delbert racing across the parking lot, followed by the angry domino players.

"There's something else too," he said over his shoulder. "It must have been an awful bad hunting season for those boys to be so jealous of one little deer antler."

We nodded, sniffed, wiped, blew, and appreciated the youngster's inference.

# Listening

"UH-OH," SAID DOREEN. We looked toward the front door. Earl and Wynona Grubbs left the summer heat and entered Doreen's 24 HR Eat Gas Now Café the way they usually do. They were arguing.

Now most married couples argue, especially those who have been married for over fifty years like Earl and Wynona. In fact, they've been married so long they're on their third bottle of Tabasco. But it isn't the arguing, it's the *way* they do it.

Wynona is hard of hearing. It's so bad that Earl has to virtually yell every time they converse. To make matters worse, Earl has hearing problems of his own, so Wynona has to shout back, even though she shouts more than she needs to since she can barely hear herself talk. After a while they become so frustrated with each other that regular conversations turn into arguments.

Their conversations are virtual scream-fests.

They took the only available booth, beside us and near the jukebox, which was booming at full volume.

"What do you want to eat!!!???" Earl asked her.

"WHAT!!!"

"I said, you want something to eat!!!???"

Wynona held out her hand toward Jerry Wayne. "Of course he looks like someone I should meet. HELLO YOUNG MAN!!!" Earl shook his head in disgust. Jerry Wayne, ever the gentleman, shook Wynona's hand. They'd known each other for years, but her memory wasn't what it was either.

"You already know him!!!"

"I DO NOT..."

The fight was on. We tried to ignore what was happening, but they were actually drowning out the jukebox. Trixie came over and talked to them for a while to settle things down. She flashed Earl a smile and I worried about his heart. Then she hugged him and I was sure it was all over. When she left I turned around to face the elderly couple.

"What are y'all gonna do this summer?" I asked.

"WHAT DID HE SAY!!!???"

Earl sighed, answered her, and then turned his attention back to me. "We're going to visit Wynona's relatives up in Oklahoma."

"WHAT DID YOU SAY!!!???"

Earl shouted back. The Hunting Club members pasted on tight smiles and tried to endure the conversation.

Woodrow had never met Earl and Wynona. I introduced him, just to stir things up for grins. "Y'all need to meet Woodrow. Woodrow, this is Earl and Wynona Grubbs. They've been married over *fifty* years."

"WHAT DID HE SAY!!!???"

"He said this is Woodrow and we've been married a hundred years!!!"

"HOWDY WINDROW, NICE TO MEET YOU! EARL'S LYING ABOUT HOW LONG WE'VE BEEN MARRIED. YOU LOOK FAMILIAR. YOU EVER GET UP TO OKLAHOMA!!!???"

Earl rubbed his forehead to ease the tension.

"I used to," Woodrow answered. "But the last time I was there I somehow made a woman mad. She laid her ears back and ripped me a new one. Said all of us Texans need to stay on our side of the river. She chewed on me for ten minutes. That ugly old woman was meaner than a snake and

had an attitude like an old sore-tailed tomcat. Wasn't much to look at, either, kinda sickly looking with yellow eyes. Had bad teeth. I bet her tongue was forked. I'd hate to run into her again. You know ..."

"WHAT DID HE SAY!!!???" Wynona interrupted and shouted across the table.

Veins popped out on Earl's forehead. He looked at her for a moment, trying to contain his blood pressure, then answered her. "He says he thinks he knows you!!!"

"I heard what he said and let me tell you something Mister Earl Grubbs ..."

We escaped out the door and went fishing. One hundred-degree heat with matching humidity was a blessing. It was quiet.

# Sad Endings

DOREEN'S 24 HR EAT GAS NOW Café was almost completely full on a Saturday morning when Tommy Lee Hanks' wife slammed the front door open and entered with the fury of a cyclone. Conversations immediately ceased when she stomped up in worn-out cowboy boots to stand in front of Tommy Lee, hands on her hips and a look so cold that Jerry Wayne shivered.

"I wasn't through yelling at you when you left!" Candy yelled.

"Obviously," Doc interjected, and then looked uncomfortably at his coffee when she turned a frigid look toward him.

First Tommy Lee tried to hide on the other side of Doc, like a squirrel on a tree trunk, but there wasn't enough room between Doc and the counter. Tommy Lee attempted to stand and face Candy, but she was so close that halfway out of his seat he had to stop in a crouch, waiting for her to step back. She remained where she was, solid as a five-foot oak. He sighed and settled back onto his stool.

A strong March wind moaned outside, giving the whole scene an eerie feeling, like something out of an old black-and-white murder mystery.

I hoped we weren't going to see a murder. Doreen still hadn't brought me the chicken-fried steak I'd ordered and any type of violence would delay my order. I was hungry.

"All you do is hunt and fish," Candy accused. "From September through February you're always off hunting something. I'd be happy if you'd stay home every now and then and just sit on the couch watching football games. At least the kids would know what their daddy looks like."

"They know me," Tommy Lee said, a pitiful attempt at defense. As homage to the Olympics, three hunters at a back table held up napkins with scores written on them; they awarded Tommy Lee's comeback a 1, 3, and 1.

"What makes you think so? Last December when you came home after deer hunting every day of your entire Christmas vacation, little Amber asked me who that bearded man was. She thought you were Santa Clause's brother."

Tommy Lee frowned. "I didn't have that much gray in my beard."

"That's not the point!" Candy raised her voice another notch. "You see, you always miss the point of our conversations." She looked around the café. "Then from March through August he's fishing."

We unsuccessfully tried to look appalled.

"I don't understand what the problem is," he said, looking around at the Hunting Club. Most of the members carefully examined coffee cups without answering.

"The house needs painting, the yard needs mowing, the city called and said your old truck is an eyesore, and I'm tired of being stared at all day long by dead animals in the living room."

"What's the *problem?*" Tommy Lee asked with a bewildered, frantic look on his face.

"I tried to understand your world. I fished with you, but you got mad when I caught that nine-pound bass last August on a North Carolina bait."

"Carolina rig," I said absently. "Hey, is that the one you brought up here and said *you* caught on a Carolina rig?" I asked. Tommy Lee ignored my question.

"Then in November I shivered with you that weekend when the water bottle froze in the stand beside us. I thought you were proud of me when I shot a nine-point buck . . ."

"She shot the nine-point you brought in on opening day?" Doc joined Candy in shouting.

Candy turned and stomped to the door. "Well that's it. I'm leaving for mother's house. And by the time my lawyer is through with you I'll have the house, the truck, the kids, the dogs, and all the furniture! You can *count* on it."

Tommy Lee, six feet, four inches, and 220 pounds of weathered muscle began to crack. His face fell. He walked to the center of the café and held his hands toward Candy. "Honey, please, whatever you do, don't take my dogs."

Candy emitted a furious little squeak and slammed Doreen's door so hard spoons jingled in coffee cups throughout the café.

"What did I *say?*" Tommy Lee asked the assemblage.

I opened my mouth and stopped. Doreen looked at me and waited. "Well, you were going to say something?"

"He had a point. Where's my chicken-fried steak?"

The boys at the back of the room scribbled their final scores and held them up.

1.3, 2, and 2.

# Firearms

**NEARLY EVERY SEAT WAS TAKEN BY THE TIME I** entered Doreen's 24 HR Eat Gas Now Café. I knew almost everyone who threw up their hands and waved. Otis Watson was there. I hadn't seen him in years.

"Otis, good to see you. How's your mama 'n them?"

"Not good, Rev. She died last week of the bloat and ..."

"Good, good. Tell her hidy next time you see her. Hello Chuck, I haven't seen you in a coon's age. How's your mama 'n them?"

The Hunting Club had possession of the large corner booth near the domino table. Jerry Wayne was reading Willie Nelson's dominos and covertly telling Delbert P. Axelrod, the Zoloft poster child, what to play in their game of Forty-two.

However, he was intentionally giving Delbert the wrong numbers so he kept playing the wrong dominos. He was losing, badly, and couldn't figure out what was going wrong with their plan. Delbert's frustration level was increasing. He made faces at Jerry Wayne, thinking no one would see.

His childish faces were making Willie Nelson mad, and he kept slapping his dominos on the table against Doreen's wishes and rules. Jerry

Wayne raised an eyebrow and rubbed his eye with three fingers.

Delbert played the double trey.

Willie won the hand and glared at Delbert.

Delbert's eyes bugged out and both he and Willie stared at Jerry Wayne who, stonefaced, acted innocent.

It was entertainment at the highest level.

"Where you been?" Doc asked me.

"Sitting in traffic," I sighed. "Everything was backed up both ways for nearly an hour."

Delbert started to make a play. Jerry Wayne frowned and shook his head. Delbert hesitated, selected another rock, and played it. Willie trumped the play.

Delbert rested his head on the table.

"Was it a wreck?" Wrong Willie asked.

"Probably a train," Patrick said. "I hate trains."

I looked at him for a moment. "I said the *freeway* was blocked. Trains don't block *interstates*."

"Well, they do if they're hauling something like the space shuttle and everyone stops to look."

I stared at him for a moment, wondering just when his brains had leaked out of his nose.

"What happened?" Doc asked.

The café quieted so everyone could hear my story. "It was awful," I said. "There was this lady driving down the highway and she decided to light her cigarette. She popped it between her lips and used her left hand to light her butane lighter. When she flicked her thumb across the wheel the lighter actually exploded."

In unison, everyone in the café drew a shocked breath.

"Flame covered her hand," I continued. "The driver's window was down so she stuck her flaming arm out the window in an instinctive move to shake the fire out."

"How awful," Trixie said. Three weakened hearts almost stopped.

"Then came the worst part," I said, after waiting for Trixie to finish, knowing everyone would be paying more attention to her.

"*Well*???" Delbert asked.

"Oh, she stopped the car and got out waving her flaming arm up and down. Traffic immediately came to a halt, and a truck driver ran up with a fire extinguisher and put the fire out. By the time I got there the ambulance had arrived and the police were on the scene."

"Poor lady," Doreen said.

"That's not the worst part."

Everyone listened.

"When the highway patrol arrived, the officer wrote the poor girl a *ticket*."

The café's occupants were outraged. Strong language was used. Ears reddened.

"What could they have possibly given her a citation for?" asked Doreen. "Her *arm* was on fire."

"Exactly," I said and got up to leave. "Willie, Delbert's cheating." He grabbed Delbert around the throat.

"Well???" Doc asked, frustrated at my story and the chaos occurring at the domino table.

"It's obvious," I reached for the door. "They wrote her a ticket for illegally stopping traffic with a firearm."

I left amid the uproar.

I just love Doreen's.

# Lucky

**DELBERT P. AXELROD, LIVING BRAIN DONOR,** sauntered through the door of Doreen's 24 HR Eat Gas Now Café leading something alive on the end of a leash.

"Get that ugly-looking thing out of here!" Doreen shouted.

Delbert stopped and looked insulted. "But it's my new dog."

I couldn't resist it. "She was talking to the dog."

Delbert frowned, trying to work that one out. "I just wanted to show off my dog. I bought him from Dave Fulson today for a ten dollar bill."

"Did you get change?" I asked.

Doc is the real dog lover of the Hunting Club. He knelt down and rubbed the dog, which immediately flopped over on his back and moaned in ecstasy.

"That's disgusting," said Doreen, watching the display by the door.

"It's disgusting because the dog is making all those noises?" I asked.

"No. It's disgusting that that dumb dog only has three legs."

"Well, Dave said this little ol' pup lost that right hind leg when he ran out in front of a Volkswagen a couple of years ago. It was broken so bad

they had to take it off."

"Awwww," everyone said.

"I've never seen a Brittany with such a short tail stub," I said.

"Yeah, he had a little problem there, too, when he was a pup. They bobbed his tail with all the other puppies, but an infection set in and they had to cut off more and more."

"Kinda mangy looking," Jerry Wayne said, looking over the back of his booth.

"I am not," Delbert argued.

"I was talking about the dog."

"Oh, well, I wish y'all would leave me alone," Delbert said. "I just wanted you to see my dog."

"And the ear?" Patrick asked.

Delbert covered his left ear with his hand. "What's wrong with my ear?"

Patrick sighed. "I was talking about the dog, dummy. What happened to his ear?"

"Got chewed off in a fight with a six-year-old Cub Scout."

The dog dozed in the floor. Several customers had to step over him to leave. Doreen was beginning to get irritated.

"I've never seen a dog with an eyepatch before," said Trixie, Doreen's redheaded waitress. We stared at Trixie with love in our eyes. Trixie is....divine. She knelt beside the dog and scratched his ear. The dog looked up at her and fell in love. He wagged his entire rear.

Many of us have considered doing the same thing to get the same attention from her.

Delbert looked at his dog affectionately. "He's had it rough. He lost the eye when some kid shot at him with a BB gun. He broke his leash and fell out of the back of Fulson's truck and was lost for four days near the lake. Poor old feller nearly starved to death before Dave found him hung up in some rip-rap by the dam. It took him a week to get over it because he was snakebit, too."

"And the toes on his front foot?" Wrong Willie questioned.

"Oversize rat trap."

"The scar on his neck?"

"Rope burns."

"Well, he's a fine dog," Trixie said and smiled. Several hearts almost required defibrillation. She gave him one last pat. The dog was so excited he made a puddle on Doreen's floor. She kicked us all outside, which I felt was unfair.

Doc looked down at the dog sitting on the parking lot. "Come on dog, let's go. Delbert, what's his name?"

"Lucky."

"Good name," Doc said as Lucky tried to dart across the parking lot in front of an eighteen-wheeler. "I hope it holds."

# Boredom

**WE WERE THINKING ABOUT GIVING UP** and going home when we began to see double in Doreen's 24 HR Eat Gas Now Café.

"I'm bored," I said to Doreen as she added coffee to my half-empty cup. I'd usually say it was half-full—*the eternal optimist*—but we were all down-in-the-mouth.

"I suppose I could arrange for a little entertainment in here for you boys, but there's nowhere to put an orchestra," Doreen said, sarcastically.

"That's not what I meant. This is a Saturday and there's nothing to do but sit in this stupid booth and drink coffee."

"He's right," Wrong Willie said, turning to Doc. "What do you want to do?"

"Drink coffee and watch Trixie. Where is she?"

"In the back," Doreen said sharply.

"I believe we might need to go, then," Patrick said.

"Where?" I asked. I sighed and envied Jerry Wayne. He snored quietly, sitting straight up in the booth beside Patrick.

"We could go fishing," Doc suggested.

"Naw, too windy," Wrong Willie said.

"Anyone want to go fill feeders?" I asked.

"I don't feel like driving out there," Woodrow said.

"Anyone care for something to eat?" Doreen asked, getting more irritated by the moment.

"Not in the mood," Doc said.

"We could go for a hike," Wrong Willie said.

"We could go to the lease and rebuild the deck behind the trailer," said Delbert P. Axelrod, a synonym for imbecile. He bumped Patrick's cup with his elbow. Coffee splashed all over the counter and dribbled downhill. I made a little dam with my hands and stopped the flow.

"That would be work," I said. "No one is in the mood to work today. We want to do something fun and interesting." I slid out of the seat and went to the restroom to wash.

"We could go out there and work on our deer stands," Delbert continued, not getting the point.

Everyone stared at our own Personal Moron. "We don't want to *work*, stupid."

"Let's take the canoes down to the Llano and go for a float trip," Woodrow suggested.

"Naw, too much trouble to organize," I called from the restroom.

Jerry Wayne snored.

"We need to get him some Breathe Rights," Wrong Willie said.

"Oh great," Doreen snapped. "Just what I need, someone sleeping in my booth with a strip of tape across his nose. Trixie! Come clean up this mess. I can't stand being around these guys anymore."

"I'm so bored I don't know what to do," Patrick said.

The café's door opened and a vision in a nurse's uniform walked in.

"Hi Dixie," Doreen said, passing her and going around behind the counter.

"Dixie?" Doc croaked.

"Yeah. I'm Trixie's twin sister."

She's Trixie's twin all right. Fate had graced the human race for once. Dixie is a carbon copy of Trixie, red hair, big—uh—eyes. She met Trix-

ie at the counter and hugged her.

"Lordy," Woodrow breathed.

Trixie just shook her head and leaned over the table to clean up the spilled coffee. Jerry Wayne opened his eyes when he finally felt the moisture soaking through his pants. "Ohhhh," he moaned. "This is the perfect dream. I see two Trixies. Did El Niño do this, too?"

They smiled in tandem. Shocked, Delbert appeared to swallow his tongue. He fell on the floor, gasping for breath.

"I need to give him mouth-to-mouth," Dixie said, her medical training taking over. She knelt quickly and pressed her lips—*oh those lips*—against Delbert's mouth.

When I came out of the restroom all five of my companions had overcome their boredom. They were all lying in a nice, neat line on Doreen's floor, hoping Dixie would hurry up with Delbert.

"I need a chicken-fried steak and hurry!" I called to Doreen.

"You must have gotten hungry all of a sudden," she responded, glaring daggers at the Hunting Club on the floor.

"No," I said, hurrying to the counter. "I'm just hoping I'll choke and she can save me, too, with that hugging maneuver."

# Flavor of
# the Day

"WHAT'S THAT SMELL?" ASKED DELBERT P. AXELROD, a rather odd carbon-based lifeform, as he entered Doreen's 24 HR Eat Gas Now Café. I followed him through the door.

Three of Doreen's patrons discreetly lifted their arms and quietly sniffed, hoping it wasn't them. One looked embarrassed and pointed accusingly at Wrong Willie, who was smiling at Trixie and not paying attention to Delbert's comment.

"That was a good one," Wrong Willie said.

Doc checked the bottom of his shoe.

"Thanks," said Trixie, taking his cup, or what passed for a cup at the moment. I noted the container was a small paper receptacle which looked as if it could hold only a jigger or two of liquid.

"What are you doing?" I asked.

"We're performing a series of taste tests for Doreen," Wrong Willie answered, patiently waiting as Trixie placed a tiny fresh cup on the counter and filled it with coffee. "Since Starbucks took coffee drinking to a new level, Doreen thought she'd experiment with different flavors."

"Try this one," Trixie said, handing me a little cup.

I sipped the sample, immediately stripping all the skin off both lips and my tongue. "Yahhhh!!!"

"Too hot?" she asked.

I gasped uncontrollably until my eyes quit watering.

"You oughta cool that first," Doc said, blowing his little cup. "I don't like this one as much as the Amaretto. Which one is this?"

"Hazelnut Creme," Doreen said, pouring coffee into everyone's sample cups. The pot was empty by the time she made the rounds of the café. Disagreements broke out among the regulars as to the preferability of the newest flavor.

"New one coming up; Irish Creme," Trixie called and began doling out the next pot. I sipped more carefully this time, even though I couldn't taste anything since most of my taste buds had been boiled.

"Yech," Jerry Wayne said. "Too sweet."

Everyone agreed.

The next pot arrived; Chocolate Mint. It immediately went the way of the dinosaurs.

A strange noise emanated from behind the counter. "What's that?" Delbert asked.

"A cappuccino machine. Lattés anyone?"

"What's a latté?" Jerry Wayne asked.

"Hot milk with a little coffee in it," Patrick answered.

Two ranch hands in the corner, Sonny Bonner and Rank Pickles, quietly covered their real-sized coffee cups with their hands lest Doreen or Trixie try to put in a latté instead of coffee.

"How about this one?" Doreen asked.

"Not bad," Doc said.

"That's Banana Creme."

Doc quietly poured the remainder into what was left in Delbert's cup, who unknowingly tossed back the mix. He would have sprayed the entire mouthful across the counter, but Doreen's glare stopped him cold. He gulped and gasped for breath.

"I don't like this one," Delbert said.

"Who cares?" Doreen snapped, losing her patience with the entire group.

I held out my empty jigger. Trixie filled it from a fresh pot.

I cautiously sipped after blowing for a moment. "This flavor is great!" I announced and offered my cup to be refilled. Without a word Trixie toured the café, refilling everyone's jigger. The consensus of the café's patrons was that Doreen and Trixie had finally hit upon the perfect cup of coffee.

Doreen was enraged. We immediately wondered what we'd done to elicit such an unwarranted response.

"What's the matter with her?" I asked Trixie, who sighed and returned the pot to the burner.

"You guys liked that coffee."

"Soooo!!!???"

"That's the same one she's been serving in here for the last ten years."

"I'd like it a lot more," said an elderly gentlemen as he and his wife left the café, "if a man could get a bigger cup of coffee in here. Those little cups just weren't enough for a real coffee drinker."

They left, vowing never to come back.

Doreen wished the rest of us would do the same.

# Justice

**SO THERE SAT ALL THE MEMBERS** of the Hunting Club, dumb-founded and howling with glee, along with dozens of other patrons in Doreen's 24 HR Eat Gas Now Café the week before Christmas.

"Justice has been served," Doc said as the ambulance left.

"I just wonder how long it will take them to open the bag again," I mused, prompting further gales of laugher.

Oh, wait, you don't know what's going on. Let me fill you in.

The excitement began when, in the course of their holiday shop-ping, John Henry and his family visited a taxidermist shop to look around. It was his lucky day. John Henry was the five hundredth person to enter the shop that weekend. His prize? An extra-large freeze-dried rattleSNAKE. Coiled to strike.

We pause here in our narrative to discuss the origin of SNAKE vs. snake. No one—*other than herpetologists who I feel need some* serious *counseling*—who ever sees or discusses a SNAKE uses the noun in a mildly descriptive manner.

Example I: "I stepped over that log over there and put my foot on a

95

snake."

See? No excitement, no power, no *emphasis*. When a man puts his foot on a SNAKE there'll be some emphasis. Believe me. Emphasis and a lot of words which are usually unprintable.

Let's try again.

Example II: "I looked down and there was a *SNAKE* right beside Earl there in his sleeping bag. You know Earl, owner of Earl's Hardware and Tearoom. Well anyway, I hollered at Earl that there was a SNAKE beside him and then I picked up a stick and whapped the bejeezus out of him. The SNAKE that is. I only hit Earl once or twice in the fray and it didn't seem to hurt him none, except he's still twitching, but I think it's more because of the SNAKE than me hitting him."

So whenever you see *any* reference to Tubular Fright—*SNAKES*—you'll understand why it's always capitalized.

SNAKES, brrrr.

Now, back to our story.

John Henry's wife took one look at the coiled SNAKE—*fangs prominent*—and emptied a plastic Foley's bag into which he deposited the diamondback. They soon headed home, but hunger got the best of them. In Doreen's parking lot a dilemma became apparent. His daughter wasn't hungry and since the day was nice, she elected to remain in the car and read.

PROBLEM: She wasn't about to stay in the car with a SNAKE, dead or alive.

John Henry's wife said the SNAKE wasn't eating with them, so the solution was to place the bag in the shade of the car, slightly under and behind the rear wheel. They trooped inside and settled into a booth, which happened to have a clear view of the car. Now everyone could keep an eye on the Foley's bag and the Major Award.

The family hadn't even received their iced tea when a new Lincoln pulled up in the lot, discharging a snooty, bouffanted lady. Apparently equipped with Abandoned Shopping Bag Radar, she spied the bag, and with moves that put the café's hunters to shame, put The Sneak on her quarry, all the time casting furtive looks to see if anyone was watching.

With a smooth, fluid motion, the woman scooped up the bag with-

out breaking her stride and entered the café. John Henry's daughter turned a page, never noticing the events that transpired outside her literary world.

Turning up her rather aristocratic nose at the café's occupants, the woman marched past the counter to settle herself at a table mere feet from John Henry's fascinated family, and directly beside the ever-present domino game. She set the bag on the floor.

John Henry slipped out of his seat, ambled over to the Club members who were seated at the counter and quietly whispered the story to us.

We turned and positioned ourselves to watch the show.

Halfway through lunch she just couldn't stand it anymore. She had to see what she'd scored in the parking lot.

The would-be thief placed the bag on the seat beside her and peered inside. Apparently her astigmatism wouldn't allow her to tell what was in the bottom. She reached for the glasses on the chain around her neck and perched the spectacles on her nose. She peeked again.

REPORT: A stuffed SNAKE-in-a-sack looks just like a live one.

With a jolt like she was hit with 100,000 volts she screeched in terror, recoiled from the bag, launched to her feet, and fell backward onto the domino table in a drop-dead faint. Dominos scattered across the floor and for the first time in weeks the game halted.

She rolled off the table onto the floor, her blue-haired head dribbled like a loose basketball for a moment. When she was out of the way Willie Nelson played the deuce-five and scored fifteen points.

The limp plastic bag closed.

Things began to unravel when a pair of off-duty paramedics joined the fray. In the confusion, John Henry couldn't just walk over and pick up something that supposedly belonging to the woman, so we watched the bag as it was deposited on the foot of the lady's departing gurney. This set off another series of shrieks from the now revived, and strapped down, individual.

"I know just how she feels," Doc said.

The café erupted, and finally the noisy trio left for the ambulance.

"There goes my SNAKE," John Henry said, sadly.

"Where are you going?" I asked Wrong Willie.

He put on his coat. "To the hospital. I've just *gotta* be there when they open that bag again."

# Hooked

**WHEN I WALKED INTO DOREEN'S 24 HR EAT GAS NOW** Café
I must have looked a little unusual since my left hand clutched a small cooler.
My right was immersed up to the wrist in ice water.

Nobody noticed.

Doreen's is like that. I stood in the doorway for a while, looking pitiful. Still no one noticed. Doreen's brother, John Albert, who is never allowed
inside the café, even opened the door for me since both my hands were occu-
pied, but he didn't say a word about my affliction.

Had he looked inside the little ice chest he would have seen a brand-
new, super-sharp, Jitterbug lure buried firmly in the ball of my thumb.

It hurt.

I thumped the cooler down on Doreen's counter. Water sloshed over
the side. She wiped it absently before finally noticing there was an alien artifact
on her counter.

"You can't bring your own drinks in here, Rev," she said.

I lifted my hand from the ice water so she could see my predicament.
The lure dangled from one end.

"That still doesn't mean that you can bring your own drinks."

"My hand is in the ice water so it won't hurt so bad." I turned toward the patrons that filled the café. "I was fishing at Anderson's Cove and got hooked. Could someone drive me to the hospital, please?"

Wrong Willie finally realized I had something hanging off my hand. "He's hooked! We've got someone hooked!"

I was immediately surrounded by patrons asking how it happened. No one volunteered to take me to the hospital.

"How deep is it?"

"When did it happen?"

"Where were you?"

"Dang, I bet that *hurts*."

I looked around. "Could someone give me a hand here?" I asked again. Three people clapped.

"Funny."

"You can get that little bitty hook out without going to the doctor," Doc advised. "Just push it on through, clip off the barb, and pull the rest of the hook back out."

I blanched.

"Better clip off the other trebles before you do that," Jerry Wayne suggested.

"You'll ruin the lure," Patrick argued. "Those things cost about four dollars."

Willie examined my hand more closely. "It's pretty deep, but I think we could just work it back out the way it went in."

"Excuse me," I began.

"I'd drive him to the hospital," Doreen told the crowd, "but it doesn't seem that serious."

"Maybe not to you . . ."

A stranger stepped up to the counter. "Were they hitting that lure?"

I stared at him without answering.

"I figured they'd be hitting motor oil colored worms this time of the year," he continued and headed for his tackle box to see if he had a similar Jitterbug.

"Lay your hand on the counter," Doc ordered.

"This isn't a hospital," Doreen said to no one in particular. "Anyone want more coffee?"

Several people produced cups to be refilled.

Willie began a story about a friend of his who had somehow managed to get the trebles from each end of a lure buried in both hands, thus handcuffing himself with a Rapala.

Even I was impressed.

"I can get it out," Harley Witherspoon announced.

My hand was still somewhat numb from the ice water, but the feeling was beginning to come back. I looked up at Doc. "Could you take me to the hospital now?"

"In a minute," he said. " I want to see if Harley really knows what he's talking about. By the way, how did this happen?"

Before I could answer Harley joined us at the counter. I wouldn't let anyone else touch my hand, but Harley reads a lot and I figured I'd give him a chance.

Willie leaned over, blocking my sight from the operation going on at the other end of my arm.

"I need your bootlace, Doc. Someone gimme a pair of pliers..."

"No! Pliers?" I shouted. "What are you gonna do with them?"

"I need them to take the lure apart. Shut up. Now, I take this bootlace and tie it around the curve of the hook," Harley said to the interested crowd watching the proceedings.

"You're using a dirty shoelace to do *what*?" I asked.

"Now, Willie, push down on the eye of the hook toward his hand, that's right, and I'll just give a little jerk."

My eyes widened. "*Jerk*? What?"

Harley sharply pulled the lace and the hook came out of my thumb with an audible pop. The café was filled with applause.

"I wanted to go to the hospital," I said, examining my hand.

"It actually *worked*," Harley said in amazement.

"You mean you've never done this before?" I asked.

"Naw. I just read about it yesterday in *Field and Stream*."

I thought about passing out. "Uh, would someone take me to the hospital so I can get a tetanus shot?" I looked at Vernal over in the corner. He's the local veterinarian. "Don't even think about getting involved in this. I need a real doctor to give me a shot."

Vernal looked like his feelings were hurt.

"Did you catch anything?" Doc asked, as he looked into my now empty cooler.

"Well, yeah, that's how I got the hook in my hand. The six-pound bass I lipped into the boat twisted and jerked the hook . . . hey you guys, where you going?"

"He said he was at Anderson's Cove!" someone shouted. Footsteps thundered out the door and everyone but Doreen, John Albert and myself headed for the lake.

I looked at my thumb. Doreen sighed. "All right. Let me get my keys. But you owe me one."

That worried me more than tetanus.

# Beepers

**"JUST WHAT THE SAM HILL IS GOING ON IN HERE?"** blustered Leroy Sikes, Precinct 3 constable. Doreen's 24 HR Eat Gas Now Café was along his usual patrol route.

Leroy couldn't get inside the men's room because most of Doreen's male patrons, several clutching fishing rods, were crowded inside awaiting their turn.

"It's Delbert's fault," several patrons announced, pointing at Delbert P. Axelrod, the mental equivalent of a newt. He was hovering around the center stall, hopping anxiously from one foot to the other, and hurrying Jerry Wayne.

"It's not *my* fault!" Delbert grumbled. "When are you going to get it, Jerry Wayne?"

Doreen stared at the crowd and went off mumbling under her breath. Trixie, who is...every adolescent boy's mental nighttime companion, smiled at the assemblage and passed foam cups of coffee through the door.

We basked in her smile. Then she returned to the counter, leaving the wounded behind.

Leroy pushed past everyone, moved Jerry Wayne out of the way and peered into the toilet bowl. "Is that what I think it is, floating in there?"

"A Baby Ruth bar," Delbert said hurriedly. "I had most of an uneaten bar in my shirt pocket and it fell in while I was trying to figure out how to get my new beeper out of the bottom of the bowl. I just got it about an hour ago."

"The Baby Ruth?"

"No, the beeper."

"Thank goodness. Now, why is your pager down there?"

"Well, my pager was delivered today at work. Then Rev, Doc, Jerry Wayne, Patrick and I were going fishing. So I came in here to change out of my slacks into some jeans, see, so I took the beeper off my belt and laid it on top of the toilet paper roll. The second I took my hand off of it the darned thing went off; it's one of those vibrating kind, and it vibrated into the bowl."

"So?" prodded Leroy.

"So now I have my first call on my beeper, it's for Emergencies Only and so I know something's wrong, but I can't find out who's trying to call me because the beeper is at the bottom of the toilet bowl and no one here will stick their hand down in there to get it out."

Leroy nodded. "I can understand that. So you sportsmen went outside and got your fishing rods to fish the beeper out."

"Right."

"I don't think y'all can do that in here. Doreen's kind of upset."

Everyone immediately produced current fishing licenses.

"Okay, guys, that's fine. What are you using?"

"A silver slab," Jerry Wayne said and jigged the pole. "I needed a deep diver to get all the way to the bottom. Rev there started with a Rapala, but he couldn't reel fast enough to get it all the way down."

"Shut up," I said and blew my coffee. "It was a deep diver. Maybe you need a rod that's a little stiffer, you know, one with more backbone."

"Hurry up," Delbert said. "Something's wrong. I need to see that beeper so I can know who to call. There's an Emergency somewhere."

Doc entered the men's room with an ultra-light rig. "My turn, I want

to try this little smallmouth spoon. You're not having any luck."

Jerry Wayne backed out of the stall and gave Doc a chance.

"I thought I had a hit," Doc said, excitedly.

"Hurry!" Delbert said. "There must be a Major Crisis at work!"

"You set the hook too hard," Wrong Willie said from his perch above the divider. He and several others were standing on adjoining bowls so they could see the action from above.

"Wait a minute," Doc said. "Got it!"

"Yea!!!"

Doc carefully lifted the beeper from the water. Delbert hurried in. To avoid touching the dripping device he twisted his head and read the number on the damp screen.

"Got it!" He hurried to Doreen's pay phone, followed by the assemblage, and dialed the number. "Hello! Hello? This is Delbert P. Axelrod. Someone there paged me. What's the Emergency!!!???"

A tinny voice answered from the receiver. "Axelrod? Axelrod? You aren't Mr. Knagg? Well, this is Beepers Are Us and we just wanted to be sure Mr. Knagg's pager is working all right. This isn't 340-6716?"

"No."

"Sorry, wrong number."

# Incriminating Evidence

**WRONG WILLIE ENTERED DOREEN'S 24 HR EAT GAS NOW** Café with a worried look on his face. The rest of the Hunting Club was already in attendance when he arrived. We noticed something was wrong when he stopped outside and spoke with John Albert, Doreen's banned brother.

John Albert is almost as bad as Delbert P. Axelrod, our personal punishment for being on this planet. The difference between them is John Albert annoys only Doreen. The rest of us kind of like him. We take him coffee outside on cold days, and occasionally try to convince Doreen to let him back in.

Come to think of it, she did let him in a time or two over the last few years, but he always makes some statement that sends her into a rage, whereupon she throws him out once again.

She won't let him back in though, because he always manages to say something about her mole or mustache. No one ever talks about either one of these strange maladies in her presence.

When Wrong Willie finally settled in our booth, no one had the

heart to tell him he looked like someone had just shot and eaten his dog.

He knew we wanted to know. He waited for a few minutes, politely, so as not to simply launch into his problem right off the bat. He could have, though, because conversation had ceased throughout the café. The only sounds were the boys playing dominos in the back and the crack when someone slapped down a double nickel and scored a dime.

"You guys have to help me preserve my sterling character," he began, seriously.

The whole café broke up. Several patrons shot streams of hot coffee through their noses at the thought of Wrong Willie even *having* character.

"Let's hear it," I said.

"Don't mess with me. It's your fault," he accused.

I was shocked. "What did I do? I haven't even seen you since we got back from our fishing trip down in Rockport."

"That's what I'm talking about. Do you remember the night we ate out at The Boiling Pot while we were there?"

Of course I remembered. We're so tight with our finances that an evening out is a memorable event. The War Department cooked supper for us before we left and sent it along, stored in Tupperware. We feasted on homemade beef stew (which I summarily scorched when we warmed it up) chicken and dumplin's (no scorch) and homemade bread.

At my suggestion we ate out one night at a seafood restaurant. The menu offered several varieties of beer. During the course of the meal, Wrong Willie tried one he'd never heard of and fell in love with it.

J.W. Dundee's Honey Brown was proclaimed the best beer in the world.

"So what's the problem?"

"I wrote the name down on a napkin, so I wouldn't forget it."

Everyone in the café leaned forward expectantly. Trixie, Doreen's fiery redheaded waitress, forgot what she was doing and leaned forward too, causing three of the café's patrons to pass out. She's usually more careful about that. Trixie is...a walking fantasy.

We propped the fainthearted back in their seats. "Big deal," said Doc. "You wrote the name of the beer on a napkin. So what's the problem?"

"Well, since Rev was trying to get our guide on the phone from the restaurant, he wrote the number down so he wouldn't forget it. Remember? You had to call several times before you got him that night to let him know we were in town. He wrote it on the napkin and I put it in my pocket."

We waited. Doreen's phone rang. She answered and spoke quietly, while at the same time trying to hear what was going on.

"The problem came when I got home. I was unpacking and the napkin fell onto the floor. My spouse picked it up and read it. Now I'm in trouble."

"I just don't understand the problem," I said. The other guys nodded in agreement.

Frustrated, Wrong Willie groaned. "The *problem* is the napkin said Honey Brown and the phone number was under the name. She thinks Honey Brown is a *woman*."

There was ten seconds of absolute silence, then we hit the floor. It was classic.

"Hey guys," Doreen called over the roar, holding the phone toward the café. "Wrong Willie's wife is on the phone. She wants to know if there really is such a thing as Honey Brown beer."

"NOOO!!!" we shouted so his wife could hear. Then we sat back to watch the results.

Never has one man talked so long and so fast as did Wrong Willie that day.

We really should tell her the truth some time.

# Freezing

**THE HEAT INDEX WAS ONE HUNDRED AND EIGHTEEN** degrees. I think that's six degrees cooler than the sun.

Idling eighteen-wheelers were making it seem even hotter. Those and the cicadas—*we called them "locusts" when I was growing up*—complaining from the nearby pecan and hackberry trees. I've thought a lot about heat over the years, mostly while sweating on a lake somewhere while hoping the fish hadn't boiled long enough to quit biting. I've come to a conclusion.

My Conclusion: It is never hot unless the cicadas are singing, so let's get rid of them, then it will be cool all the time. It has to be the bugs making it so hot, because the more they sing, the hotter it gets. It's genius, isn't it?

The blacktop parking lot of Doreen's 24 HR Eat Gas Now Café was fuzzy from the shimmering heat waves. My glasses immediately fogged when I opened the truck door to step outside. I was afraid the soles of my tennis shoes would melt before I got inside. If that happened the little bubble of air in the hi-tech sole would pop and there I'd be, stranded in the sun with a flat.

That scares me some. What do you do when your tennis shoe gets a flat? No one I know carries a spare, unless it's some woman with a suitcase-sized purse. Who do you call to fix a tennis shoe flat? Who repairs it? Would someone show up with a hydraulic jack and have to lay on their back under my shoe to plug the leak?

I could just see myself abandoned, leaning slightly to the side with a neon yellow sticker slapped across my glasses, warning me to move or be towed.

There are a lot of things in this world to worry about.

I stepped through Doreen's front door and almost went into shock. My glasses frosted over and chill bumps broke out on every part of my body. My shirt, wet from sweat, suddenly became cold and clammy.

Once again Doreen's proved that Texas in the summertime is the coldest place on earth.

"Shut the door!" Doreen and Trixie shouted in unison. Shocked, I slammed the glass door, just missing Wrong Willie's foot as he headed outside.

"The door-closing thing-a-majiggie is broken," Trixie explained. "All the cold leaks out."

"Good," said Doc. The Hunting Club was huddled together for warmth in the large corner booth. They shivered in unison, like a nest of Chihuahuas.

"Dang, it's cold in here," I said.

"It's summertime," Doreen explained, as if I hadn't noticed the furnace outside. She was wearing a sweater. "I have to keep the café cool for my customers. They expect it."

I looked outside. Wrong Willie draped himself across the hood of his truck, soaking up sunshine like a lizard.

Doreen poured hot coffee into everyone's cups. They extended blue hands and wrapped them around the warm cups.

Several sighed in ecstasy.

"It was this cold in the movie theater Friday night," Doc said. "I wasn't thinking and wore shorts and a T-shirt. I darn near wound up

hypothermic. My better half took a sweater and she was fine."

I continued to watch Willie through the window. He was rummaging around behind the seat of his truck.

"I've seen women carry blankets into the theater in August so they wouldn't freeze to death," Jerry Wayne said. "I heard they had to chip a lady out of her seat with an ice pick the other day."

Willie came back into the café and stopped all conversation. He wore his insulated camo hunting jacket. In his hand was a duffel. We blessed him as he pulled out sweaters, gloves, ski caps and other cold-weather items. Five minutes later everyone was layered up in hunting clothes. Doc was a picture, sitting there in shorts, a camouflage wool sweater and a stocking cap.

If you didn't know better you'd think it was January.

Roscoe Hightower, a local rancher, came through the door and settled himself at the counter. Trixie poured him a tall glass of iced tea and he nodded toward us.

"There they go again. I've known boys who like to hunt, but this bunch is always a little too excited about opening day."

We shivered, smiled, and sipped hot coffee.

# Retirement

PATRICK ENTERED DOREEN'S 24 HR EAT GAS NOW Café
with a grin so wide he nearly had to turn sideways to get through the door.
The rest of us looked at him, annoyed. He was far too cheerful for such a
hot day.

Patrick slid into the booth next to Doc and grinned even wider at
everyone, like he knew a secret. "You're bothering me," I said.

"I know why he's in such a good mood," Doc said. "He's officially
retired."

It was true, and that annoyed us even more. Patrick was the first
member of the Hunting Club to reach retirement age. He was free. Free to
sleep late, to lounge around the house in his rattiest underwear, to drink
coffee at night to stay awake and watch sordid infomercials on late-night
television.

He'd achieved The Dream.

"Your job is to find us a new deer lease, then," said Wrong Willie.
Our current deer lease wasn't panning out.

"I won't have time," Patrick said.

Go Home, work out, Don't Drink.
Don't Smoke, NO SEX, AND you'll
LIVE to BE 90.

How Do you get By with Smoking...
AND Drinking AND The Like?

CAUSE I'M A DOCTOR.

We stared at him for a minute. "You're *retired*," Jerry Wayne said, slowly, thinking maybe Patrick didn't fully understand the concept of retirement. "You don't have anything *but* time."

"Nope. I'm buying a lake house and it'll take all my time to get it fixed up."

"You don't need a lake house," I said. "If you want to go fish we can always go to Doc's place on the lake. Why do you need another one?"

"Because I can sit on my own porch and look at the water."

"You won't have time to do that," Jerry Wayne said.

"I won't?"

"No."

"What'll I be doing?"

"Looking for a new deer lease," Jerry Wayne answered.

Doc slowly spun his coffee cup in place, thinking aloud. "Y'all leave old Patrick alone. He's retired now, so he can do anything he wants, you know. The old codger can sit on the porch in his rocker if he wants to. You go ahead on."

Patrick frowned. "I'm not *that* old. And I didn't say anything about rocking chairs."

"I guess when you reach retirement age you have to slow down," I agreed. "Maybe putter in your flowerbeds some, or you could take one of those basket-weaving classes to keep your mind active. It'll keep your fingers from stiffening up."

"Well, my shoulders *have* been a little sore," Patrick agreed, shrugging his shoulders and rotating an arm. "But I don't feel older."

Doc squinted at Patrick. "Numbness? You do look like you have a little more gray in your hair, too."

We all looked at Patrick's hair. It was completely gray and had been for the past several years. We pondered the obvious.

"Don't put yourself out," I said. "You don't want to do too much in a day's time."

"What are you talking about? I can still get around."

"Retirement should be great, though maybe after 60 your hearing isn't what it used to be," Doc said, trailing off at the end of his observation.

"Huh?" Patrick leaned forward, missing the last few words.

"Just like he said," Jerry Wayne grunted. "Losing your hearing. Maybe you better just let us try to find a lease from now on. When we find one we can help you to your stand in the mornings and come for you every evening."

"Maybe I don't look good," Patrick thought aloud. "But I think I feel all right."

"Go on home," I said. "Get your rest."

Patrick straightened up in the seat. "You guys are wrong. I feel great! Tell you what. I'll finish up at the house and then start looking for a new lease. By the end of August we'll have us a new place. Leave it to me." He threw a dollar on the table, and when he worked the stiffness from his knee, he almost trotted out of the café.

I looked at Doc. "Good thinking, Doc."

He grinned. "Why do you think everyone started calling me Doc?"

I'd always wondered about that.

# Impending Wedding

**DOREEN'S 24 HR EAT GAS NOW** Café was rapidly filling with hot outdoorsmen. The outside temperature was hovering in the uncomfortable neighborhood of 102 degrees. Doreen was unusually snappish about hunters holding the door open too long.

The jukebox thumped out the latest country and western hit. Willie Nelson sat in the back, playing dominoes with three members of the local Spit and Whittle Club. It was common courtesy observed by Doreen's patrons to leave Willie alone and not bother him for autographs or inane fawning conversation.

"Craig is getting married," Doc announced to the members of the Hunting Club. "They're getting ready to set the date."

We dutifully looked at Craig and shook our heads sorrowfully. He grinned sheepishly and nodded agreement. "Karen says you can all come. We're not ones to have one of those long engagements, so we've decided to get married this weekend."

A horrified gasp went up from the crowd. The jukebox took that instant to end the song. Even Willie stopped his domino game for a moment and waited for the result of such an earth-shattering announcement.

I cleared my throat in the silence. "Have you discussed the date with anyone here?"

Craig frowned and looked at the café full of shocked faces. Doreen scowled and refilled my coffee cup.

"Stay out of this," she ordered.

"What's wrong with the first of September?" Craig asked.

Jerry Wayne put a hand on Craig's shoulder. "Has it occurred to you that dove season is open and the first full weekend is traditionally the time everyone hunts after a long dry summer?"

"I'll only miss one opening day for this year, and then I can hunt with you guys from then on."

Hoots and derisive snorts filled the café.

"Boy, are you green."

"He don't know what he's getting into."

"He'll learn, the hard way."

"Think about it. You'll have an anniversary falling on that date for the rest of your life," Doc said. "No, sorry, the first weekend in September just won't do. You'd better decide on some other time."

"I'll have to wait until dove season is over. I guess the first weekend in October will work."

"Nope," I said. "That's when squirrel season opens, and some of the best camping time all year is in October."

We drank coffee and thought in silence. Willie played a domino and made a nickel. "How about November? The boy has to get married some time. Y'all can't just leave him hanging."

"November won't work," interjected John Albert, Doreen's brother. He'd behaved himself so well in the past that she had just recently allowed him to sit at the end of the counter, but only if he stayed out of the way and didn't irritate her. "You don't hunt deer, but we all do, so that's out."

"Quail and turkey season open then too," Doc thought aloud. "December is out because of Christmas, so I guess January is the month."

"That won't work," Craig said. "Our family always goes skiing in January. By the time we get back we're out of money."

We thought about it. Doreen "harrumphed" her way down the counter, pouring coffee and occasionally splashing it on the hands of those she was most irritated with.

"I can't believe you guys just sit here and tell this poor boy what to do with his life. Has it occurred to you his future wife might have something to say about when *she'd* like to get married?"

Everyone looked at the floor and felt sufficiently chastised.

"February?" asked John Albert. Doreen shot him a look that would have killed any normal human being, but John Albert was like an old dog that had been bitten by SNAKES so many times he was immune to the venom. "WHAT?" he asked in exasperation.

"It's the only month," I agreed. "March, April and May are out because we're either skiing, fishing or hunting turkey. June is the traditional month for weddings, but isn't that when we're all planning to go to the Red River to fish for trout?"

"August," said Delbert P. Axelrod. "Nothing is happening in August. It's too hot to fish, and no seasons are open yet."

"That's it!" Doc agreed. "Craig, you get married in August. It's the best time."

"But August is a year from now," Craig objected.

"August is better than February," I said and drained my coffee cup. "Doing it this way will give you a year to get ready and by that time you can tell whether she'll like hunting and fishing. It's the perfect time."

Craig got up to leave. He hesitantly put his hand on the door and stopped. "You're sure?"

I nodded. "We're sure. Trust us, we know what we're talking about. Besides, if she says anything, just tell her it was Delbert's idea."

Everyone nodded and held out empty cups to Doreen. She mumbled something under her breath about raising ostriches for a living.

"Honey, we can't get married this weekend because dove season just opened. We'll have to wait until next August," Craig said, using the door for practice. He nodded, straightened his shoulders and went off to meet his destiny.

# Mushrooms

**PLEASE SIT DOWN FOR THIS HEARTWRENCHING** tale of experimentation and woe.

For some reason known only to Delbert P. Axelrod, one of life's little stumbling blocks, he decided to cook a venison steak dinner for the entire Hunting Club and their wives. Luckily, I didn't arrive until later in the evening.

It all began when Delbert felt the need to cook venison smothered in mushrooms. As usual, he put off planning the event until 12 hours before dinner. Delbert had everything but the mushrooms.

And the A&P was out of mushrooms, fresh or canned.

I happened to be at Doreen's 24 HR Eat Gas Now Café that morning when Delbert came in, whining about his dilemma.

"Why don't you use some of those mushrooms Doreen picked last night down by the creek?" I said, just to mess with him. "She uses them here all the time and I bet she'll sell you enough to cook one meal."

Delbert's dumb, but he isn't stupid. "You can't eat those kinds of mushrooms; they're called toadstools and they'll kill ya."

Doreen came out of the kitchen, we explained the problem and Delbert left with the mushrooms—*store-bought*—and a little niggling in the back of his mind. Since he still wasn't sure if they were really the safe mushrooms, he decided to try an experiment to be sure.

At home Delbert cooked up the mushrooms and gravy, poured it over a piece of venison steak and fed it to Blue, his new coon hound. Then he watched the dog all afternoon to be sure he wasn't suffering any ill effects from the meal.

By suppertime Blue was just fine, so Delbert felt safe and cooked up a fine meal of venison smothered in mushroom gravy and served it to everyone there. The Hunting Club members and their wives pronounced it the best meal they'd ever eaten.

I was late and they were all finished with the meal when I arrived. I came in through the back door after witnessing a disturbing sight, and decided the best thing was to tell Delbert what I saw right away. Everyone was sitting around the table, finishing their iced tea—*the men fiddling with their tobacco pouches*—and talking.

I walked through the kitchen door and into the dining room. "Delbert, I just came in through the back yard. Old Blue is dead."

For a period of three heartbeats the room was graveyard silent. Then I couldn't have gotten more of a shocked response than if I'd thrown a live skunk onto the table.

"YAAAHHH!!!" screeched Delbert. "Nobody move! Stay calm!" He jumped for the phone and began to frantically dial. I couldn't believe everyone was so upset about Blue, but to allow them some time to vent their grief, I went back into the kitchen to make my plate.

The following occurred while I was there. Delbert called the paramedics and told them he'd poisoned everyone with toadstools. The head Para advised everyone to stay calm, but there wasn't enough time to get everyone to the hospital. They would send help.

Minutes later two ambulances screeched to halt in front of the house, spraying it with gravel and flashing lights. The paramedics jumped out with their arms full of equipment and ran into the living room where they found everyone calmly laying on the floor like Pick-Up Sticks. Without a word they grabbed the nearest victim, pulled him into the master bedroom and pumped his stomach.

Minutes later he staggered out and the paramedics pulled in another victim, then another, and soon every member of the dinner party was back in the living room with freshly pumped stomachs.

Then the paramedics left and everyone sat around, limply, blinking at each other.

Meanwhile, I heated up my mushroom gravy smothered venison and ate in the kitchen. But I couldn't get over what I'd seen outside. I came back into the living room just as the front door closed.

"You know," I said, noticing that everyone looked a little peaked. "What I can't get over is how that car out on the road never even slowed down when it ran over old Blue."

Now everyone's mad at me!!! Sometimes people are so weird.

# Memories

**TYPICALLY THE LADIES DON'T GET AS EXCITED** about new tires as men do. I noticed this lack of vulcanized excitement when Leroy Dance arrived one evening at Doreen's 24 HR Eat Gas Now Café.

Male customers stopped outside to lean over the sides of Leroy's old '55 Ford truck to talk tires. Trucks have a knack for solving the class system of male discussions. The Round Table design allows participants to equally converse across the bed.

We were heavily into the Tire Discussion portion of male bonding when Delbert P. Axelrod, who would look good strapped across the hood, arrived just in time to spoil the rest of the day.

Delbert rested one jeaned cheek on the tailgate and barged right into the conversation. "I thought you guys were talking about something good when I saw y'all looking over the side. Shoot, there ain't nothing in here but a bunch of bailing wire and hay."

"We were talking about Leroy's new tires, Delbert," I answered. I usually try to ignore Delbert's existence, but I was feeling pretty good, what with Leroy's truck sitting on new shoes and all.

Delbert examined the tires. "Shoot, these tires are the best part of this old heap now. Leroy, why don't you sell this wreck and buy a truck that will go with them tires?"

Several of us backed away from the anticipated killing. Leroy never twitched. "Well, Delbert, my daddy gave me this old truck. It's worth a lot more than you think."

Delbert didn't have enough sense to let it go. "Just look at this paint job, and all these dents. Man I'd just use this on the deer lease."

I practiced my shallow breathing, hoping that when Leroy went into a blind rage he wouldn't notice me standing nearby and shoot me for simply knowing Delbert.

Leroy casually reached out, grabbed Delbert's ear with a callused thumb and forefinger, and led Delbert's watering eyes around to the front. "Come here. See that crease in the bumper, next to the right headlight? I put it there when Daddy was teaching me to drive. I hit a cultivator when I was trying to remember where the brake was.

"These scratches along the fender and door are a matched set with the other side. I got them the night Rev and I were flying down a dirt road in Lamar County and didn't turn when the road did. We plowed through a barbed wire fence and stopped nearly a hundred yards deep in a pasture full of Brahman bulls with attitudes. We spent the night in the cab."

Delbert's eyes began to cross. He was led toward the cab. "That dent in the door there perfectly fits the side of my head. On my twenty-first birthday the girth broke on my saddle while I was chasing a calf.

"About all that's left of the driver's seat is a scrap of material and a couple of springs. Dad wore out the material. I'm wearing out the springs."

Delbert's eyes bugged out like a mouse in a trap.

"Dad and I installed the gun rack when I was about eight. He carried his .22 rifle in the top rack, and my BB gun always rode in the bottom."

Still gripping Delbert firmly by the ear, Leroy pulled him around to the passenger door. We scrambled out of the way.

"Daddy put that crease in the door when his eyes got so bad he couldn't properly judge distance. The gate by the barn wasn't quite as wide as he remembered."

"See this, Delbert?" He pointed at a dent surrounded by dents.

"I think," Delbert answered. "Do you want me to?"

"Those scratches came from the night Bobbie Lynne and I were dating and I backed into a ditch when we both should have been home. I stopped the truck before it went completely into the ditch, jacked up the right rear bumper, and when she gunned the engine forward, I shoved the truck off the jack and it caught the back fender. I'm lucky it didn't knock my fool head off. We drove off on our honeymoon in this truck."

Leroy completed his tour by returning Delbert to their starting point. "With Daddy driving I shoved hay over this tailgate from the time I was big enough to walk. Then when I was grown, my boys did the same when they were still in diapers. Bobbie Lynne was convinced they'd fall off and get killed, but I told her no one ever died from falling into cow paddies.

"I've cleaned birds on the tailgate, hauled deer home in the bed, and have carried friends from one field to another on opening day of dove season. I like this old truck. It has a lot of memories. And if you don't annoy me any more, you can live to have a few more memories and dents, too."

Delbert rubbed his newly liberated ear. "Nice tires."

"Thanks."

# New Truck

**I KNEW IT WASN'T GOING TO BE A GOOD DAY.** Wrong Willie was suffering from the male version of PMS, I'd burned all the skin off my tongue with a hot cup of coffee and had forgotten to look left, right and then left again when crossing a street. An overloaded Winnebago ran me down, interrupting my peaceful contemplation as I stood in the street and examined a fresh armadillo carcass.

Why do they always come to rest with all four feet sticking up?

Delbert P. Axelrod's truck pulled up in the parking lot of Doreen's 24 HR Eat Gas Now Café. Delbert climbed down several feet from the cab and stood there admiring his jacked-up four-wheel ride. The Hunting Club sat inside and watched as he walked around the truck, polishing invisible smudges and checking for oil leaks.

Delbert, whose head is so empty you can blow into one ear and put out a match on the other side, is worse than a two-year-old with a fresh sucker. He sighed happily, pointed the automatic door lock transmitter toward the truck and pushed a button.

Immediately the security alarm activated in the "panic" mode. Lights

flashed, the horn honked and a deadly blue aura of electricity surrounded the secured vehicle. An emotionless robot voice could be heard over the clatter of dishes in Doreen's.

"Get away from the vehicle! Step away from the vehicle!"

Delbert jumped in shock and furiously pushed buttons on the transmitter. The alarm finally stopped.

He self-consciously walked to the café, staring at the treacherous device in his hand. Once inside he pitched the keys on Doreen's counter and waited for the inevitable.

Wrong Willie got right to the point. "Why did you get an alarm system on that thing? They only go off in the middle of the night. If it did start shrieking in the daylight, it would probably be while you're in a deer stand somewhere and the only living things that would hear it would be you, the deer, and a few rattleSNAKES."

"It's part of the anti-theft package I bought. Truck thefts are rising."

The shriek of Delbert's alarm resounded through the café. He jumped up, ran out the door, and shut off the alarm with his remote transmitter.

Jerry Wayne glowered at him when he came back in. "I hate those things. They go off all the time and no one ever pays any attention."

"Not true," Delbert said defensively. "If someone tried to steal my truck the alarm would scare them off."

"It would only make them work faster," I said.

"Don't touch the ride!" shouted the truck. "Back off!"

Delbert looked surprised. "That's part of the package. You can select any warning from a list of about ten alarms, but I didn't pick that one."

"I hate that bull," Doc growled.

Delbert rose again, slower this time. Apparently several false alarms required less enthusiasm.

The alarm shrieked again. "Y'onta go turn that thing off for me?" Delbert asked Jerry Wayne.

"I will if I can use a baseball bat."

Delbert slouched back to the truck.

"You could strip a car while one of those things screamed bloody murder and people would think you were just trying to find a way to shut it off," Doc said.

"Do you know anyone who can say a car alarm has prevented a theft?" I asked.

"I turned the sensitivity down," Delbert said when he came back in.

A Buick Roadmaster pulled up beside the truck and when a Little Old Blue Haired Lady emerged she bumped Delbert's truck. Immediately a shrill alarm began to sound.

"WEEEEE!!! WEEEEE!!! GET AWAY FROM THE VEHICLE!

WEEEEE!!!"

Panicked, the little old lady headed for the café at a dead run. Doreen caught her at the door and settled the victim into a nearby booth. I took two-to-one on a heart attack.

"Shut *that thing* off, Delbert," she snapped. "Rose's dentures will chatter for a week because of that thing."

"I bet you parked in the handicapped space again, didn't you?" I asked.

He looked up in shock. "Oh, no. I forgot. How did you know?"

"'Cause your ride is leaving," I replied.

"WEEEEE!!! GET AWAY FROM THE VEHICLE. STEP BACK!!! WEEEEE!!!" screeched the truck as the tow truck pulling Delbert's pickup turned onto the highway.

"I was wrong," Wrong Willie said. "The alarm does work. You can tell when the truck is being stolen."

"WEEEEE!!! PUT ME DOWN!!!"

"I hate those things," Wrong Willie reiterated.

Everyone agreed.

# On The Air

"PUT THE MICROPHONE OVER THERE AND WE'LL use the booth by the counter," said the man with a mellow voice.

The Hunting Club looked up from its careful examination of Wrong Willie's most recent injury. He'd been finned under the thumbnail by a large angry catfish, who was because of this minor indiscretion, now residing under twenty pounds of ice in a cooler in the back of Willie's jeep.

A group of men bearing sinister-looking sound paraphernalia entered Doreen's 24 HR Eat Gas Now Café like they owned the place. We'd been invaded by one of those talk radio programs broadcasting from a "remote" location.

"Outdoors Today," with host Barney Peet, had selected Doreen's for the Saturday morning broadcast. In minutes they were ready. After a brief sound check Barney smiled at everyone in the café, shook our hands, and settled in behind the microphone.

He placed a set of headphones over his ears and at precisely ten o'clock he was on the air. "Good morning! This is Barney Peet and you're listening to 'Outdoors Today.' " (Big fanfare music.) "We're broadcasting live from Doreen's 24 HR Eat Gas Now Café."

"Last time I heard him he sounded like he was broadcasting dead," Doc said to Jerry Wayne.

Peet looked at them, annoyed, and continued. "I heard about this café a few weeks ago because it has earned a reputation with local out-doorsmen who stop by to eat and share their outdoor experiences."

We looked at Wrong Willie's rapidly swelling thumb. "Sharing out-door experiences," Doc repeated.

Barney looked around the café. "I'm surrounded by rugged indi-viduals who love the outdoors and they've dropped by here to share with us their campfire tales, hunting stories and strategies for catching more fish."

"We have?" I asked no one in particular. "I just wanted coffee and to watch Wrong Willie's thumb swell." Wrong Willie held the thumb up for everyone to see, hoping for sympathy.

Three new café patrons came through the door, saw the thumb in the air and responded with their own "thumbs up," apparently thinking Willie was happy about the broadcast.

Barney stopped for a commercial and during the break urged us to become involved with the broadcast. Doreen shook her head at his reckless request and sighed. Barney saw Willie's thumb in the air and gave him a thumbs up in return.

Willie frowned.

"Welcome back," said Barney, after the break. "Let's talk fishing and structure. As you all know, structure is essential to locating fish and I'm sure some of these fishermen here have their own theories. Let's get some input and hear how they use structure for productive fishing."

He waved at Delbert P. Axelrod, a man who's not *totally* worthless because he can usually serve as a good bad example.

"Sir, what's your favorite structure? Drop-offs? Brushpiles? Creek channels?"

"Yugos."

"What!!!???"

"Yugos. You know, that ugly little car they used to import from

Yugoslavia? Well, there's this Yugo about a hundred yards off Wind Point in about ten feet of water. There's always a bunch of bass and crappie hanging out there, and usually a catfish or two."

"Thanks," said Barney, looking around frantically. "How about you? You seem to be a happy individual; giving me a thumbs up and all. What's your name?"

"Wrong Willie."

They stared at each other. Willie's thumb stood in the air, apparently with a mind of its own. It throbbed quietly. Silence, save for the hissing of the airwaves, emerged from the monitor speakers. "Thanks," he waved toward the next person at the counter. "Your name?"

"Reavis."

"You made that up. Hey, you, what's your name?"

"Jerry Wayne."

"Great. A real name. What type of structure do you prefer?"

"I prefer old tires, but I've learned to appreciate the finer points of sunken washing machines."

There was thirty seconds more of silence. For a moment Barney looked like he'd eaten a live marine animal. They went to break. The remainder of the morning's broadcast originated from the hardware store down the street.

"Should I have said sunken refrigerators?" Jerry Wayne asked, looking out the window at the broadcast truck in the hardware store parking lot.

"He must be some kind of purist," I answered and tuned Doreen's radio to pick up the remainder of the program. I wanted to know if refrigerators were better, too.

I noticed Willie's thumb and returned a thumbs up of my own.

# Sunburn

**DOREEN'S 24 HR EAT GAS NOW** Café was packed with fishermen cooling down from a broiling summer sun. Heat waves shimmered above the black asphalt parking lot.

I gingerly stepped into the cool interior and broke out in goose bumps. At her customers' request, Doreen keeps the thermostat set somewhere near Eskimo Cold.

Immediately upon walking through the door I held my arms out from my sides and slowly made my way to an empty counter stool beside Doc. He turned and stared at my sun-reddened face and arms.

"Get some sun?" he asked. Doc is a master of the understated question.

I nodded miserably. "I was fishing down on the river and fell asleep in the shade."

"I've never seen anyone burn so bad in the shade," Patrick said as he walked up and slapped me on my shoulder.

A shriek that sounded like someone eating a live cat filled the café. Patrons stopped and looked around, searching the booths to find out who

had the nerve to order a live animal. I realized the shriek had come from my own throat.

"I went to sleep in the shade. But when I woke up the shade had moved."

"Did you catch any fish?" Wrong Willie asked, looking up from the domino table.

"I'm dying here, and you're asking me about fish."

"I just wanted to know if it was worth going out in the heat. I'm staying in here if they're not biting."

The refrigerated air caused me to shiver. Doc looked down and noticed my legs. "Did you sleep with your pants off, too?"

"No," I answered in my most pitiful voice. "But when I woke up there was this dang SNAKE asleep with his head in my lap. I jumped up to run away and ran straight through the biggest bull nettle patch south of the Red River. Now my legs itch and the rest of me burns."

Trixie, Doreen's waitress, leaned over the counter and looked at me with her big, soft eyes. The general agreement among the Hunting Club is that Trixie is...dazzling.

"Can I do anything to make you feel better, hon?"

Before I could answer, Doc butted in. "Don't give him an opening like that, Trixie. Besides, I've got the sure cure for his bull nettle. I'll be right back."

Doc left the café and rummaged around under Greenvan's seat. We watched him through the window while other patrons in the café suggested cures for my sunburn.

"My granny used to put fresh cream on a sunburn," John Henry suggested. "Doreen, do you have any cream?"

"None that I'm going to let him rub on his body in here," she answered.

I brightened up. "Trixie could do that for me."

"No," Doreen snapped.

"She has those little cups of powdered cream," suggested Delbert P. Axelrod, the man with the road-kill brain. I glared at him.

"If someone had some aloe vera plants we could smear the juice on his burns," Jerry Wayne said.

"Trixie could do that for me," I said, again.

"I said no," Doreen re-emphasized and wiped off the counter. "No one is going to rub *anything* on *anyone* here."

Doc returned with an aerosol can. "Take your pants off."

"Not in my café!" Doreen shouted. "People are trying to eat."

"Doreen," Wrong Willie said, "people have eaten in here while we've performed minor elective surgery. A little spraying won't hurt anything."

"I don't want anyone undressing in my café; the Health Department will close me down."

I looked pitiful. My bottom lip quivered.

Trixie frowned. "Go ahead, Doreen. I can't stand to see Rev suffer."

She finally relented. "At least go to the bathroom to do it."

I headed for the bathroom, followed by nearly a dozen café regulars.

"The vice squad will probably show up now," Doreen grumbled.

Once in the bathroom I dropped my cut-offs and Doc sprayed my legs. The itching immediately stopped.

I was amazed. "What is that stuff?"

"Windshield de-icer," Doc answered, idly reading the can.

An elderly gentleman emerged from one of the stalls and stopped, staring at one man with his pants around his ankles, another spraying something on the above-mentioned itchy legs, and both surrounded by a dozen onlookers, holding their coffee or iced tea.

He didn't even slow up to wash his hands. "I don't want to know what you boys are doing," he said and hit the door. "Eighty-six years old and until this moment I thought I'd seen everything."

At least my legs are better. What's good for sunburn?

# Stingers

**"I NEED SOMEONE TO GO HUNTING WITH ME** Tomorrow,"
Doreen said to the members of the Hunting Club gathered at her place,
Doreen's 24 HR Eat Gas Now Café.

"It's July," Doc pointed out. "This is fishing season. There's no hunting in July."

"There is where I'm going. There's pass shooting and still shooting.
If you're any kind of a wingshot you guys will keep busy for a couple of
hours."

"May as well," I said. "There's nothing else to do."

Such statements get me into trouble all the time.

Doc, Patrick, Wrong Willie, Delbert P. Axelrod, our personal penance
for living in this century, and I, met Doreen the next day at lunch. She
loaded us into her Suburban. "You guys leave those shotguns here, I'll sup-
ply everything you need." And we drove to an old ranch house in the country. She stopped on the gravel drive and we got out.

"This is my new home," she said, rummaging around in the back of
the car. "I just bought it last week." She passed out cans of wasp spray. "No

one has lived here for about two years. Yellowjackets and wasps have almost taken over and I'm allergic to stings, so I thought you guys would enjoy helping me."

"Uh, oh," Patrick said and backed off, shaking his head.

Wrong Willie and I grabbed cans of spray. "Let's go. We'll take the interior."

Doc frowned at a can of waspicide in his hand. "C'mon Delbert. We'll look around out here."

Patrick slammed and locked the Suburban's doors. "I'll keep the air-conditioner running."

Willie and I stopped in the doorway of the large living room and looked around. "I don't see any bugs," I said.

Willie looked my way, gasped, and directed a stream of bug killer at my head. I ducked and the blast soaked an enormous yellow-jacket nest barely two feet from my cap.

The angry insects were already hot and mad before we ever started shooting. I think they sleep all swelled up, wings extended, standing on their toes. They dropped off the nest like yellow leaves and charged us. We backed into a corner, alternately shooting and ducking. One got through our defenses and nailed Wrong Willie just above his eyebrow.

It immediately swelled shut, drastically impeding his aim.

"YAAAA!!!" In the middle of the battle Delbert came running through the house, hotly pursued by a swarm of red wasps. His head looked like a lumpy water bucket from several stings.

Wrong Willie shot at Delbert just for good measure.

"You're supposed to be outside!" I shouted at his retreating back.

"I'm going!"

Another nest of yellowjackets in the corner of the living room began to discharge its occupants into the fray. Soon the room was filled with a cloud of noxious chemicals, apparently lethal only to humans. The insects seemed to thrive on the stuff. I was convinced they were getting a rush off the insecticide.

We slowly backed toward the doorway and into the yard, fighting for every inch. Delbert was draped over the hood of the truck, pounding weakly on the windshield in a vain attempt to get Patrick to unlock the doors to let him in. A cloud of red wasps swirled over his prostrate body like a mini-tornado.

Patrick responded by turning on the wipers.

Doreen and Doc hunkered in the shade of a large pecan tree and watched the proceedings with interest. Doc occasionally directed a stream of insecticide at passing wasps by leading them a foot or two, usually dropping them with the first blast. It reminded me of dove season with him laughing and pointing.

My eyes watered from the chemicals we'd sprayed into the air. No wasp could come any closer than five feet without dropping dead from the fumes emanating from our clothes.

"You guys want some first aid and a drink of water before you go back?" Doreen asked.

"No," I said. "Just some matches. We're gonna burn the house down and rebuild. It'll be safer for everyone."

Patrick waved at us from inside the air-conditioned Suburban, and pushed the windshield washer button just to aggravate Delbert some more.

He seemed pleased at the results, as Delbert rolled limply off the hood, and happily turned up the radio as he waited for us to complete Phase II of our assault.

# Stress

**DELBERT P. AXELROD, WHO CAN MANAGE TO STEP** on every rod in the boat as he moves from one end to the other, came walking through the door of Doreen's 24 HR Eat Gas Now Café; backwards.

Doc looked up from his examination of Woodrow's suddenly bloody thumb. "This is going to be good."

I really didn't care about Delbert walking backwards. I was more interested in Woodrow's thumb. Where there was once a rather innocuous little wart, a large seeping hole now opened his thumb to an examination of several inner layers of skin and tissue.

We'd been sitting in the booth, talking, when Woodrow dug out his knife and began to shave at the wart, kinda like whittling. The only difference is that wood shavings don't bleed.

I watched for a while, fascinated, while he carefully shaved the wart down. Jerry Wayne covered his coffee cup with his hand, to prevent wart shavings from getting into his drink.

The shaving was progressing nicely, everyone felt, until Delbert came through the door in such a strange manner. Woodrow looked up, did

a double take, and cut a little too deeply.

"Dang!" Woodrow yelped.

Delbert stopped beside the table, whirled around and stamped his foot. "Woodrow, I went to your stress relief speech the other day and decided that my life was too stressful. So now I'm doing odd things to relieve stress."

Patrick snorted. "He has to *think* about being odd?"

The door flew open behind Delbert and an excited young boy ran in. "*Mama's been shot!!!*"

Doreen immediately dialed 911 and we were out of our chairs and into the hot parking lot in a flash. The boy pointed to a green Buick. A lady was leaning over, her head resting on the steering wheel. "What happened?" I asked the boy.

"We just went to the grocery store and stopped by here to eat. When we finished and got back in the car Mama rolled down the window and someone shot her."

Doc leaned into the open window and shook the lady's shoulder. "Lady, can you hear me? We have an ambulance on the way. Can you hear me?"

"Yes," came the muffled voice. "I've been shot in the back of the head."

"Don't move," Woodrow shouted, dripping blood from his thumb onto the side of the car.

Delbert twirled a few times, hysterically chanting. "Stress relief, stress relief."

"Keep talking to me," Doc said, gently holding the lady's hand. "I don't see any blood. Where were you hit?"

Constable Hubert Flaws powerslid into the parking lot and ran to the car. "Good Lord, look at all the blood on the outside of the car."

"That's mine," Woodrow said.

"Are you hurt, too?" Hubert asked him.

Delbert twirled. Everyone else ignored Hubert.

"Talk to us," Doc said to the injured woman.

"I was just sitting in my car," she said weakly, "when I heard the shot and felt the impact against the back of my head. When I reached back I felt my brains leaking out. I'm hurt so bad there's no feeling back there."

Doc examined the back of her head. "I think you'll be all right."

"Are you out of your MIND!!!???" Hubert shouted at Doc and then turned to Delbert. "Hey, you, quit whirling."

Doc reached out and removed a gooey substance from the back of the woman's head.

"Ohmygosh, Doc just picked up the woman's brains!" Delbert shouted and began jumping from one foot to the other.

"The bathroom is inside," Hubert told Delbert. "Put that woman's brains back," he ordered Doc.

Wrong Willie examined the substance. "This isn't brains." He sniffed. "This is buttermilk biscuit dough. Pillsbury, I think."

I looked into the back seat. The intense heat in the closed car had caused the canned biscuits to explode, splatting against the woman's head.

The ambulance took that minute to roll up and the paramedics jumped out. One attendant headed toward the nauseous Delbert laying on the ground, and the other went to the more obvious wound; Woodrow's bloody thumb.

The embarrassed woman drove quickly away.

I looked around the parking lot at Delbert, who was now being whapped on the head by one of the paramedics.

"*Now* what's happening?" I asked Doc.

He shrugged. "Delbert got so dizzy spinning around that I told him he could get rid of the nausea by putting his head between his knees. But he got mixed up and tried to put his head between that paramedic's knees."

I willed my heart to slow down. "Woodrow, I think we all need your stress workshop."

"I think this hurts, too," Woodrow said to the pretty female paramedic.

I chewed quietly on the biscuit dough.

# Stretched Truths and Outright Lies

**WHEN THE WHITE-HOT SUMMER SUN BEATS** mercilessly down on the sometimes-uncovered heads of suffering outdoorsmen they, like cattle, seek shade. Our shade this time wasn't under a shade tree. It was in the form of the cool interior of Doreen's 24 HR Eat Gas Now Café.

Doreen would have run us all out years ago, but for some reason she prefers the company of most outdoorsmen and ranchers to that of the traditional highway-weary tourist. One of her favorite pastimes is watching us scare her patrons. Sometimes we even engage in a little tourist-baiting just to pass the time.

"We couldn't fish today without being covered up with SNAKES," Wrong Willie said. Immediately several tourists ceased the tinkling of tea-spoons and paused to better hear our discussion.

Willie swiveled his stool away from the counter and addressed the Club members in a booth behind him. "Me and Jerry Wayne," everyone duti-fully looked at Jerry Wayne, asleep in a booth with his mouth slightly open, "were out on the lake this morning, kinda plugging away at some lilypads near a creekmouth, when this old waterSNAKE swam by with a half-grown frog in his mouth. Well, I got to thinking, we weren't doing much good with artificials, and if SNAKES were hitting frogs, maybe bass would too."

"So when the waterSNAKE got close enough I scooped him up with a net and tried to get the frog out of his mouth. He wouldn't let go, and I didn't want to kill him, so I grabbed the SNAKE by the back of the head and tried to pry the frog out of his mouth with a pair of forceps."

Jerry Wayne shuddered in his sleep, no doubt reliving the story in his subconscious. Doc, who hates SNAKES with a passion, joined him in a sympathetic shiver.

"That old SNAKE still wouldn't let go, so when Jerry Wayne wasn't looking I snuck his bottle of SNAKEbite medicine out of his tacklebox..."

"SNAKEbite medicine?" asked a fascinated tourist.

"Yeah, you know, he had half a pint of J.T.S. Brown bourbon in there," Wrong Willie said, disgusted at the ignorance of the man and his interruption. "Well, anyway, I opened the bottle in my right hand with my teeth while holding the SNAKE in the other, and then I carefully poured a good slug of whiskey around the frog and into the SNAKE's mouth."

"He immediately let go of the frog, and I pitched him overboard. That old SNAKE thrashed around in the water for a good five minutes before he disappeared underwater in a swirl of bubbles. I threaded the frog on my hook and tried to fish, but I had to give it up."

"Why?" asked a thoroughly hooked tourist.

"Well, by the time I got that frog on my hook I couldn't cast for all the SNAKES around the boat offering up frogs for trade." We hit the floor laughing.

The tourist grinned at how well he'd been taken. "I've never had trouble with SNAKES, but the last time my partner and I went out we caught something you boys have never hooked in your lives."

"What's that?" I asked.

"Me and M.D. were fishing a large lake just outside of Dallas late one night when I hooked something that bent my rod completely double. It felt like a Buick on the other end and it took me nearly thirty minutes to land it, since I was only using eight-pound-test line and didn't want it to break off."

The members of the Hunting Club nodded knowingly.

"I finally hauled my catch up close to the boat and reached down to lip him in when I saw what I'd caught."

We leaned forward expectantly.

"What *was* it?" Doc asked.

"Well sir," the tourist looked around. "I'd done gone and caught myself a *body*, the body of a *dead* man, bobbing there in the dark beside my boat."

We shuddered in horror. Jerry Wayne shuddered a second time in his sleep and muttered, "SNAKE, body."

Brrr.

"What did you do?" Doc asked.

"Why hell, we were into catch and release so we threw him back. We caught five more the same size before the night was over."

We sat amid the laughter, stunned that we'd been reeled in so easily by a stranger. The man smiled, paid his ticket and walked toward the door. "I'll see you boys later."

"What makes you say that?" I asked. "We don't even know you."

"I always wind up seeing everyone sooner or later," he said. "I'm the new mortician in town. Like I said, see you later."

The entire café shuddered in unison, chilled despite the brutal heat outside.

# Adopt
# -A-
# Highway

A LINE OF PARKED VEHICLES belonging to the Hunting Club sat hub-deep in the summer-dried grass alongside Highway 243. It was a cool October morning and the Club members were standing around with a dozen or more of Doreen's regulars, sipping coffee supplied by Doreen's 24 HR Eat Gas Now Café.

Doreen had decided, all on her own and without input from any of us, to adopt a portion of Highway 243 and keep it free of litter. We had told her no.

We couldn't say no, though, when Trixie asked us, because Trixie is...resplendent, and for that one shining reason we'd do anything—walk through fire, or even be friendly to IRS agents—for her.

So there we were, watching Trixie climb out of Doc's new Dodge Ram. Doreen had just finished pouring fresh coffee in our Styrofoam cups when Trixie slipped out of the cab, causing several of the café's regulars to gulp the contents and suffer second-degree burns from the scalding coffee.

Hubert Wells was so overcome with emotion that he squeezed his foam cup a little too hard and it exploded. He hissed with pain, sucked his damaged fingers and never took is eyes off of Trixie. He could have burned his entire hand to a crisp and wouldn't have given any more response.

A passing eighteen-wheeler slowed almost to a standstill to watch her walk along the roadside. Brakes screamed in torture behind the truck as other drivers tried to avoid rear-ending the semi at the same time they watched Trixie.

Doreen passed out empty plastic trash bags to everyone in attendance. The bags were white with orange lettering advertising Doreen's Café. "This is great advertisement for the café," she said. "Adopt-A-Highway programs keep business names in the public eye and are good for the environment, too."

"Speaking of eyes," Doc said. "Trixie, come here

real close and look. I have something in my eye big that's as big as a hedgehog."

Doreen's own eyes narrowed as she continued. "Everyone take a bag and we'll start picking up trash. I've adopted this section all the way down to County Road 2224."

I looked at the expanse of road fading into next week. "This is going to take all morning," I complained, catching a movement from the corner of my eye. Jerry Wayne reached into his truck and pulled out a .22. "Where are *you* going?"

He put a finger to his lips. "I just saw a couple of squirrels in those trees. I'll just be a minute."

He crossed the five-strand barbed-wire fence, loaded the rifle and went hunting. I picked up a discarded foam cup. The coffee that dripped out was warm. "This is ridiculous! I'm picking up our *own* trash before we can even get started. Look, it says Doreen's."

Delbert P. Axelrod, the man with the intelligence of a three-day-old roadkill, stared down at his feet. "Do we have to pick up the dead animals, too?"

Wrong Willie joined him. They knelt to examine the hairy object at their feet. "This isn't a roadkill."

Patrick leaned over. "That's Earl's toupee (*Remember Earl's Hardware and Tearoom?*). He's been looking for it. He and Thelma got into an argument last week and she got so mad she pulled off his rug while they were driving down the road and threw it out the window. Earl's had to wear his cap all week. Pick it up and we'll take it back to him."

"Uh-uh," Delbert said. "I'm not touching that nasty thing."

A commotion by one of the trucks caught my attention. Three people were using whatever was handy to vigorously whap something in the grass at their feet. I went over to take a look. By the time I got there Woodrow picked up a recently—*very recently*—deceased SNAKE by the tail.

Doc's enthusiasm for the day's activities suddenly evaporated as if someone had turned off a switch. He virtually leaped into the truck cab. "I'll drive alongside you boys and you can put your full trash bags in the back."

Doreen was getting angrier by the minute. "Are any of you guys going to help me with this?"

"I'm trying," I said. "But everything I've picked up so far has Doreen's written on the side." I held up another foam cup.

A shotgun blast startled everyone. "Dang it!" Jerry Wayne shouted from the woods. "What are you shooting at? I'm trying to hunt squirrels here."

Across the fence, Patrick reloaded his shotgun. "I couldn't stand all these dove flying over without getting a shot or two."

I picked up another cup and happened to glance back down the highway. Cars stretched off into the distance, slowed by Trixie in her jeans. Horns honked and exhaust was a blue cloud rolling toward us.

Someone in a waiting car threw out a cigarette butt. Another dropped a paper cup out the window. The dry grass caught fire and began to burn toward the parked trucks.

"So much for the environment," I said to Doreen and hurried toward my truck.

"That'll take care of the SNAKES," Doc said, smiling broadly.

Doreen glanced up at the Adopt-A-Highway sign and stifled a sniffle.

She should have known better.

# Trapping

**THERE WERE PROBABLY FIFTY INNOCENT PEOPLE** eating in Doreen's 24 HR Eat Gas Now Café when an inhuman and unearthly screech of fear and loathing wafted from the kitchen, rolling over the counters and tables like a physical presence.

The café became silent, waiting for another screech.

"Something's eating Delbert!!!" Jerry Wayne shouted gleefully, not realizing Delbert P. Axelrod, a prime example of why some mothers should eat their young, had already left the café. "Yea!!!"

"I bet she finally tasted her own chili," Doc offered. "I still think she uses road-kill in it."

"She probably looked into a mirror and finally noticed her traveling mole," Wrong Willie said.

Ask six people where Doreen's mole is located, and you'll get six different answers. This phenomenon has baffled scientists in white lab coats for years. They boil colored water in strangely shaped beakers while nervously fingering calculators without coming up with a single satisfying clue as to how the mole travels at will.

The Hunting Club simply takes her mole as a matter of course.

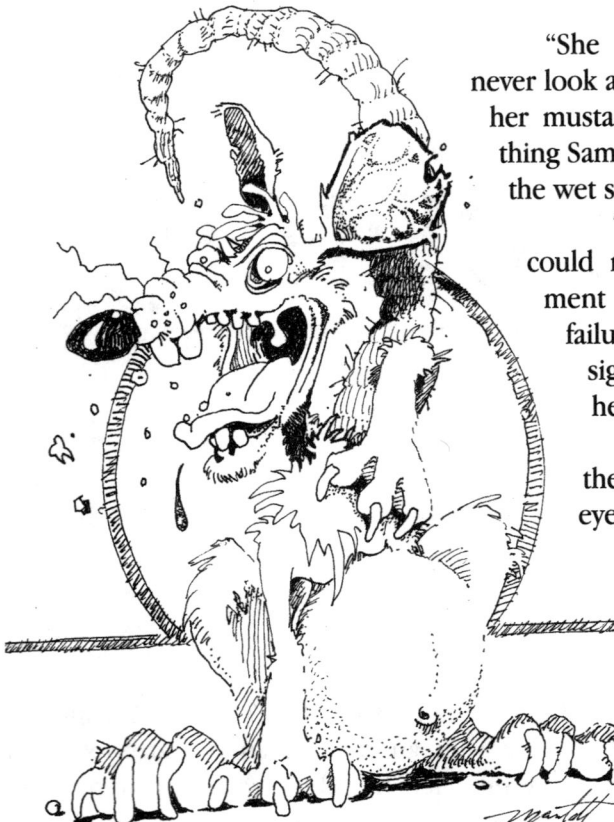

"She probably realized she'll never look as good as Trixie, because her mustache is thicker than anything Sam Elliot could grow during the wet season."

Trixie is ...superb. They could make an entire ER segment centered around heart failure induced by the mere sight of The Perfect Redhead.

Doreen flew into the café, a wild look in her eyes. "You boys go get your guns! Flame-throwers! Nuclear devices! Kill it! Everybody! I want big guns, with lots of ammunition!"

"You gonna shoot Delbert?" I asked, hopefully. Maybe Jerry Wayne was right.

"No! I'm gonna shoot the giant rat I just saw in the pantry."

Suddenly the café patrons consisted of only five customers. Myself, and the other four members of the Hunting Club. The stampede to evacuate the café looked like sand flowing through a funnel.

"Now that we're such an intimate little group," Doc said, "why don't you tell us what happened?"

Doreen settled onto a counter stool and fanned. "I was in the pantry, to get some crackers, because that's all you guys usually eat when you just drink coffee and talk. I can't keep them in stock. When I picked up the box I saw it had been chewed. Then a rat the size of a *baby* crawled out of the box, *slithered* over my hand, and disappeared through a hole behind a five pound can of nuts."

Everyone shivered. Brrr. It's amazing what one rat can do to men who've hunted all their lives.

"What do I do?" she asked.

"Sell the place," Trixie immediately interjected. "Now." She hates rats.

"Get some traps," I suggested.

"Yeah, big steel traps, with teeth. The kind that look like little bear traps," said Wrong Willie with an excited glint in his eye. We call him Wrong Willie because everyone confuses the name with Willie Nelson, one of Doreen's most famous domino-playing regulars.

"Good idea," Doc agreed. "Put the box of crackers back on the shelf. Then set one trap by the crackers and the other trap by the nuts. You'll catch him."

"Sell the place," Trixie repeated, concerned. She kept staring at the kitchen door, no doubt imagining a mutant rat was going to saunter through the swinging doors and belly up to the counter while calling for coffee and cheese.

"It won't take long," I said. "If your rat is brave enough to be out running around during the day, you'll have him before closing time."

"It isn't *my* rat. I just want him dead." She also looked toward the closed kitchen door. They stared together. "One of you guys will have to take him out of the trap for me. I'm not touching that nasty thing."

"You said the same thing the first time we brought Delbert in here," Patrick reminded her.

"We'll remove the carcass," I ignored Patrick. I was getting excited about a hunt, even if it was trapping for rats in Doreen's. We were through with dove season for the most part, and I hadn't been in the mood to hunt squirrels because ...

"We'll stay with you," said Patrick, interrupting my reverie. "This is better than going home to watch my wife burn supper again."

Jerry Wayne grinned from ear to ear. "My favorite is the satisfying sound a snapping trap makes."

Doc and I departed the premises in search of rat traps. We located just what we wanted at Earl's Hardware and Tearoom. We purchased two mini bear traps and returned to the café. Doreen still hadn't re-entered the kitchen. She and my confederates were lurking around the counter, waiting for the traps so they could act out their sociopathic fantasies.

I love those guys.

We smeared peanut butter onto the trigger and set the first trap beside the crackers. Doc's mouth froze in painful shock when the trap snapped shut on the middle digit of his right hand.

"Jeeze!!!" he shouted through gritted teeth and held up his injured appendage. "I hurt my finger."

"That's not a nice thing to do," I informed him, miffed at the sign language.

He continued to hold his injured digit aloft, whimpering softly to himself. I set the other trap beside the nuts, near the hole. We carefully closed the pantry door and returned to the counter to await retaliation.

"Where did you put the traps?" Jerry Wayne asked. "If you didn't put them in the right place the rat will miss them."

"Shut up. We know how to stake out trapping territory," Doc answered and held up his injured finger. "I hurt myself, too."

The boys responded to his gesture with one of their own.

Doc frowned. "Well, we put one by the crackers and the other one by the nuts, just like Doreen told us."

His response seemed to suit everyone. Bets were taken on the successful trap. It was three to three, with Trixie abstaining. She called us incorrigible.

"I can't wait for the results," Doc said. Half an hour—*and six cups of coffee*—later the satisfying sound of a trap snapping shut filled the café. Applause all around.

Doc went in to check on the deceased. He returned, stifling a snicker.

"Got him," Doc answered and held up the deceased rat. With a pitiful moan, Trixie fell out. Doreen eeped and stifled a gag.

"Well?" I asked, annoyed by all the commotion. There was money on the outcome of this trapping expedition. "Did you catch him by the crackers?"

"No," Doc answered, barely containing his laughter.

Doreen summoned her courage. "Well?"

"It's obvious. If we didn't catch him by the crackers, we had to catch him by the nuts," he said.

And that's how we found ourselves banished, standing outside on the parking lot, debating whether to hunt or go home.

I still don't know why the girls got mad.

# Remodeling

DOREEN PLOPPED A MAGAZINE on the counter beside my cup. "I want to remodel this place. What do you think?"

I eyed the color photograph. The café in question looked like a tea room, complete with lace curtains, rusty antique farm implements on the walls—*we used to call them junk*—and neon lighting.

"You want this place to look like that?" I asked, looking around me at the Formica counters and tables, and the farmers and outdoorsmen slurping coffee. "We wouldn't feel right in here."

"That's what I had in mind. I was looking to attract other folks, too." She sighed and rested her chin in her hand.

Trixie looked over her shoulder. "That's a little too foo-foo for these guys. What about something with a little different look, but with the same flavor?"

We all looked at Trixie with love. She understood outdoorsmen.

Doc joined the conversation. "This type of remodeling will cost a fortune, Doreen. Why not let all of us pitch in and help you? All these boys are good at something, whether it's woodworking, or painting or whatever."

"Yeah," John Henry said. "Just close down for a few days and let us get after it. You'll love the results."

Doreen looked at Trixie. "I'm probably losing my mind, but it sounds like a good idea. It's the labor that costs so much. All right, here, take this magazine and use it for ideas, and I want a different look over there . . ."

The Hunting Club and a dozen regulars took a couple of days vacation from our *real* jobs and met early one Thursday morning in front of Doreen's 24 HR Eat Gas Now Café. Several trucks rolled up and parked, disgorging rump sprung truck drivers.

Doc ran the show. "All right, guys, here are the plans. Doreen wants a cozy, family-looking place so people will think they're home when they stop to eat. That's what she'll get."

"Who brought the deer mounts and the stuffed fish?" I asked. More than one man hurried to a truck and returned with a trophy that had been gathering dust somewhere at home. "Let's do it!"

We worked almost nonstop through the days and nights so we could finish the job before Doreen returned.

The interior of the café was ripped out to the studs. Before we were finished, the only thing inside the building was the floor. While one team did the interior work, the second gave the exterior a face-lift. Two more days were required before we finally finished at dusk. As the sun slowly settled behind the café a week later, the lights snapped on, bathing Doreen's café in a warm, neon glow.

The squeaky old wooden sign was gone, as was all the scuffed linoleum, the tired Formica counter, the worn booths and broken seats.

The exterior now looked like a hunting lodge, down to the log front. Peeled posts held up a sloped porch roof and braced the two by sixes that served as banister rails and seats for those who wished to sit outside and talk for a while.

It was a café that brought a tear to every outdoorsman's eye. Warm wooden paneling covered the walls; an oak counter greeted the eye upon entering the café, and wooden tables lined the walls under plate glass windows. But that was only the start. A restored Wurlitzer—*courtesy of the Schneider drivers*—bubbled happily at the far end of the room, directly behind a new domino table. Willie Nelson's donation.

Recessed lighting was located throughout the restaurant, strategically positioned to light the 12-point buck Doc had shot several years ago. An 11-pound bass was mounted directly over a new neon sign that said "Welcome." Quail, duck, goose, pheasant, and turkey mounts filled the walls and brought color to the café.

In one corner, just to the left of the door, was a recessed cabinet, full of antique fishing rods and wooden lures. On the opposite corner a similar cabinet held proud, worn shotguns. Between them were shelves full of books on hunting and fishing.

The floor was tongue and grooved oak, courtesy of the local lumberyard. Behind the counter was a cook's dream of new and refurbished coffee makers, grills, stoves, and cooking utensils, everything donated by Doreen's customers.

Doreen and Trixie drove up to watch us put the finishing touches on the building. They were shocked to see that we were through. Doreen stood, open-mouthed, in front of the café. Suddenly we became nervous. Five minutes into the remodeling we'd thrown out Doreen's magazine, drawings, and most of her ideas in a frenzy of creativity.

Now we wondered if we'd gone too far.

Too late.

Doreen walked slowly to the front door and looked inside. "I asked you guys for new counters and lace curtains. I wanted wallpaper with little ducks and farmers on it. Trixie, look what they've done," Doreen whispered, her eyes filled with tears.

Embarrassed and uneasy we followed the girls into the café. Doc cleared his throat. "I'm sorry Doreen, but we just got carried away," he trailed off.

"Look, Trixie, there's nothing here that I asked for. I've never seen anything like this." She walked through the café, lightly touching everything with her fingertips as if she couldn't believe what she was seeing.

Trixie's face was blank, but still beautiful. Several of the boys began to slowly back toward their trucks, hoping Trixie wouldn't remember they'd been there.

The girls looked at each other and began to cry. Now we really knew we were in trouble. "It was Delbert's idea," I said, resorting to a tactic that had saved me numerous times when I was a kid. "He's the one who came up with all this stuff. We really wanted to do it like you said."

"Delbert," Trixie turned and hugged him. "This is perfect. We didn't know anything could be so wonderful. Our idea wouldn't have worked out here, but this will bring in people from everywhere. You're a *genius*."

She kissed him. Trixie *kissed* Delbert P. Axelrod. It curled *my* toes.

Doc hit me with his cap. Jerry Wayne retched.

Now Delbert eats there for free. It's the story of my life.

I never know which way the wind is blowing, but I have a feeling it's always blowing toward Doreen's.

We hope to see you there soon.